A FALLING STAR

A FALLING STAR

•

Carolyn Brown

AVALON BOOKS
NEW YORK

PRINTED IN THE UNITED STATES OF AMERICA
ON ACID-FREE PAPER
BY HADDON CRAFTSMEN, BLOOMSBURG, PENNSYLVANIA

With love to my daughter Amy.
For all the love, encouragement, and support—here's your book!

Chapter One

Retta King made a big red bow and wrapped it
around the poinsettia pot. Red blossoms—gold paper,
red bows; white blossoms—silver paper, green bows.
Holiday colors for the Christmas season. She pushed
back her long, blond curls and wiped a bead of sweat
from her brow even though it was freezing cold outside and threatening snow.

She shut her eyes tight and visualized a rambling,
old house covered with sparkling Christmas lights,
snow falling, a big green tree with gaily wrapped
packages underneath and the smell of hot, homemade
bread baking in the oven. Her mother, with blond hair
like her own except for a few strands of silver peaking
through here and there, was basting a turkey. Her father, a short, stocky man with dark hair and twinkly,
blue eyes, sipped coffee while he watched Country

Music Television from his favorite, well-worn, brown leather recliner.

"And there were poinsettias in every corner," she muttered as she fluffed the bow and set the plant in the window with two others.

'What was that Retta?" a soft, southern voice arked from the back of the shop. "Something about a corner?"

"Just me mumbling when I should be appreciating every one of these poinsettias that we sell," she raised her own southern voice so it would carry back to her great-aunt. "Goodness knows whatever is left next week, we sure can't sell and we certainly can't eat them."

"No, we can't," Anna, her great-aunt said with a giggle. "I'll put on a pot of water and we'll take a break with raspberry tea and that shortbread we got from the salesman. He always brings the best tin of shortbread at the holidays, doesn't he?" Anna wasn't a bit taller than Retta's five feet two inches, but she was almost as wide as she was tall. Her hair was a faint shade of blue this week. Some weeks it was purple, some weeks it was a rich gray. As she said so often, "Sometimes the hair dresser gets it right. Sometimes she doesn't. It doesn't matter anyway. It puts a little spice in my life."

"Tea sounds wonderful," Retta said as she picked up a spool of bright, hot pink ribbon and eyed the white leaves on the poinsettia plant. It wasn't a Christmas color and would probably sit in the shop until after Valentine's Day, but if she had to make another red or green bow she would be sick. She chose a pale pink, irridescent paper and set the pot in the middle of it, gathered it up at the four corners and wrapped the bright pink ribbon around it.

"Looks beautiful," a deep voice startled Retta from behind. "Sorry, I didn't mean to scare you," he said. "I guess the bell isn't working," he said as he looked back toward the door.

"I guess not," she said, blaming the breathless feeling on the fact that he'd scared her. "Want to buy it?"

"No, but it is beautiful. A person gets tired of red and green at this time of year," he said, showing off beautiful white teeth behind firm lips, a deep dimple on the left side of his face, and a cleft in the middle of his chin. "I need to place an order to be sent to Claremore, Oklahoma. I hope it's not too late to get it there by tomorrow evening," he said as he cocked his head to one side and stared at her with his mossy green eyes. Retta could have waded in his eyes and happily got lost for all eternity plus three days. They were as soft as new grown grass at the first of spring and as twinkly as a falling star.

"We can do it," she said with a smile. "Claremore is a pretty big town so it shouldn't be a problem. Do you want a poinsettia wrapped in pink?"

"It's tempting, but I better do the traditional thing this year. I want a dozen red roses," he said with a big, bright smile. "I'll sign a card." He picked up one from the circular display and looked around until he saw a pen laying next to the cash register. He wrote his message hurriedly and shoved it inside the envelope. "How much?" He looked up into the palest blue eyes he'd ever seen. They were the color of a cloudless summer sky—the kind of eyes that a country singer could make a whole song about.

Maybe tonight he'd go back to his apartment, get out his guitar, and compose a song about a blue-eyed girl who made pink instead of red bows for Christmas. Norman would have an acute cardiac arrest if he wrote a best–seller in the three months he was going to be in Nashville. Good old Norman had been here seven years and was still struggling to get his foot in the music door.

"They're high this time of year," Retta replied. This was probably another one of those fellows who sold everything he had and came to Nashville with music notes and dollar signs in his eyes and very little in his pocketbook. "Do you want the roses in a box with a ribbon or in an arrangement?"

"Arrangement," he said. "One of those big, clear cut glass vases with sparkly marbles in the bottom and some of that white stuff—baby's blanket?"

"Breath," she said with a chuckle. "Baby's breath."

"Yes that's it and that fern stuff in it too. Nothing's too good for my darlin' Emma," he said as he smiled and laid a crisp one hundred dollar bill on the counter top.

"She must be special." Retta rang up the amount and began counting back change. "Not every girl gets that kind of arrangement on Christmas Eve."

"Not every girl is Emma." He smiled again and Retta's heart flip-flopped in her chest. "Merry Christmas, Miss Anna," he said, setting his gray felt cowboy hat on top of his thick, pérfectly styled black hair, and tipping it toward her.

Retta replied, "Merry Christmas to you." She didn't tell him that Miss Anna, the proprietor of Miss Anna's Florals, was her great aunt.

His tight Wranglers fit like second skin and were starched to perfection with a perfect crease. They bunched up around his boot tops like they were supposed to and the mossy green leather in his bomber jacket matched his eyes perfectly. As Retta watched him get into his white pick-up truck and drive away she thought she wanted a man. He was the kind of man she might be drawn to someday who made her catch her breath just looking at him one, who knew how to dress, and one who sent roses because nothing was too good for Emma.

Emma didn't know what a lucky woman she was. It was Retta's all-time dream to live in Claremore, Oklahoma, to have a man send her an arrangement of roses that cost almost a hundred dollars, and to sit

across a dinner table and look at someone so handsome that it just plain took a woman's breath away.

Retta sighed loudly. "How beautiful!" Aunt Anna
said from so close behind her she jumped for the second time in less than fifteen minutes. "Who would
have thought of pink for Christmas? If no one buys
that, I'll take it home. Are you ready for your tea? Did
I hear a man's voice up here? Was it Brett?"

"No, it was a customer. I've got to call an order in
to Oklahoma, Aunt Anna, so please set my tea over
there," she said and nodded toward the counter top
where he laid his card. She picked up the phone and
leafed through the book, finding the florist they did
business with in Claremore. She gave the order and
then took the card from its envelope to read the message to the lady on the other end of the phone. "Sign
the card, 'Merry Christmas, Darling Emma.' He
picked out a standard Christmas enclosure card. Oh,
and that's with a capital 'D' on darling also." Retta
fought back another sigh.

"Good sale," Aunt Anna said as a half dozen
women rushed in the front door.

"We need a dozen poinsettias for table center
pieces," one lady said. "Oh my, isn't that pink one
gorgeous, and it would match the theme for our make-
up convention. Could we possibly have a dozen like
that in two hours? We're having a holiday make-up
convention and we forgot all about center pieces for
tonight's dinner. We've got a million other little er-

rands to run, but we could come back in a few hours if you could fix them up just like that," she chattered, still admiring the pink concoction Retta thought would still be in the store when there was nothing left but a few leafless sticks instead of a lovely plant.

"Of course I can," Retta said. Today is your lucky day; I have thirteen more white poinsettias.

"Then make all thirteen," another woman said. "With that one right there, it'll be fourteen and I want two for my dinner party at home tomorrow."

"Wait a minute," another said. "I've got a family gathering tomorrow too. But I want red ones. Could you do something creative—maybe a red-and-white gingham check since my house is pure country? I'll take six to flank around the fireplace guard."

"Me too. I want four with black bows and paper," another said.

"Whew," Retta said as she let out a whoosh of air when the women paid their bills and dashed back out into the cold wind. "Guess we'd better get busy if we're going to get all this done in two hours, Auntie. I guess we're not going to have to eat any of these plants after all. When we're done there will be one lonesome old red girl left and that's all."

"And you'll be so rotten tired you won't even enjoy your party tonight," Aunt Anna said and picked up the pink ribbon and started making bows with the expertise of a long-time florist. "Is Brett going to be there?"

Retta rolled her eyes.

"Don't you roll them eyes at me, child," Anna scolded. "You're twenty-six-years old. Years ago you'd be considered an old maid. Goodness knows I was at your age. Soon you will be left with either divorced men with kids you'll have to raise or else the leftovers no one else wanted. At least Brett doesn't fall into either of those categories."

"Yes, but he's just a friend and he's . . ."

"He'll find out soon enough that he's not country music material and he'll find a good job and propose to you," Anna said firmly. "Hand me that staple gun and make that black bow a little bigger. Can you believe someone would want black ribbon on a Christmas poinsettia? Next year I'm ordering twice as many and dressing them up in the wildest colors imaginable. We may make a fortune. Now let's talk about the party."

"I'd rather not," Retta muttered. "Brett isn't my type and he'll be standing on the strip with a Karaoke machine when he's eighty-five-years old."

"No he won't," Anna argued. "Bet that good lookin' fellow who gave you the order for the roses will be back in," she said with a glimmer in her old blue eyes. "He looked like he could lean right across that counter and kiss you."

"Don't tease me, Auntie," Retta said with giggle. "Why did you ask if it was Brett if you already knew it wasn't? Besides he's got a girlfriend in Claremore. His Darling Emma, according to the card."

"So. All's fair in love and war." Auntie Anna winked. "And Claremore? Your dream place in the whole world."

Retta didn't want to go the Christmas party. She didn't want to fight with her long, curly blond hair and try to tame it into a style that made her look like a woman rather than a sophomore in high school. She really didn't want to wear her new tight blue jeans or put on make-up. She would much rather pull on her soft, red-flannel night gown and curl up with a good book and a big bowl of popcorn. Now, that was an evening to envy, and not a house full of noisy people all talking about whether or not they were just seconds away from a recording contract.

Retta promised her friend, Lila, she'd be there. Lila begged Retta to pick up her house key at the Grand Ole Opry where she was performing and even though Retta knew it was just a ploy to get her to the party, she went along with it. Retta would get to Lila's early and be there to oversee the caterers and light Lila's eight million candles so everything would be glowing when the crowd arrived. With a heavy heart, she grabbed her hair brush, pulled all the shoulder length blond curls up into a twist, roped it down with one of those new red plastic clips, and fluffed her bangs with a twist of the comb. "There," she looked at her reflection. "I'm an old maid at twenty-six and not a teeny bopper at sixteen," she mumbled as she applied a minimum of make-up.

She parked her sixteen-year-old blue Chevy truck in the lot, shoved her hands down into the pockets of her denim jacket, and berated herself for forgetting her gloves. At least she didn't have to walk very far. Lila was portraying the late, great Minnie Pearl tonight and she was supposed to be fairly close to the entrance. People milled about everywhere, snapping pictures, waiting in lines, talking, and laughing.

The whole affair depressed Retta. She'd cut her teeth on the Grand Ole Opry. She knew most of the stars personally. Many of them had been close friends of her parents until two years ago when they both died in a freak automobile accident. People came here with glitter in their eyes, ready to meet the stars, anxious to get an autograph, a photo or even to buy a T-shirt to prove they'd really visited Nashville. What Retta wanted was a fast train out of this place, a knight in shining armor to arrive on a white horse and carry her off to a magical kingdom close to Claremore, Oklahoma—a place she lived and fell in love with after six short weeks. Retta dreamt of the two of them living happily ever after, watching the beautiful Oklahoma orange sunsets, and loving each other every day.

"And the moon is made of green cheese. Mars is populated with funny lookin' people with antennas sticking out of their heads. And there's some oceanfront property over by Graceland. I could sell any one who believes all that," Retta mumbled to herself. "Besides those things only happen in the movies when Richard Gere and Julia Roberts are the stars. It does not happen in real life."

"Hey, Retta," Lila called from a circle of other young people, each of them dressed like a Grand Ole Opry star. "Over here." Lila waved and Retta smiled, but it didn't reach her eyes. Lila was almost six-feet tall and had long, straight brown hair which she shoved up under a made to order Minnie Pearl wig she'd bought. Her nose was just slightly too long for her face but she had the softest doe-colored eyes in the whole state of Tennessee.

"Got that key?" she asked as she joined the group.

"Sure, right here," Lila pulled off her black Mary Jane shoes, just like Minnie wore in all her performances, and took a house key out of it. "Don't snarl your nose, girl. It doesn't stink."

"Don't bet on it." Retta laughed and this time her eyes did twinkle a little.

"Aren't you going to introduce me, Lila?" a man asked so close behind Retta that she could smell his woodsy after-shave. She whipped around to find the man who'd ordered the roses; he was standing so close she could see how deep the dimple on his cheek depressed when he smiled. He was a Bill Anderson lookalike that night, dressed in a red Nudie suit, complete with sequins and 'Hi!' embroidered inside the front of his jacket.

"Oh sorry, Denison meet Retta," Lila said in a rush. "Now the caterers will be there in half an hour," she rambled on, "you don't have to do a thing, just make sure all the candles are lit when they are finished. We'll all be there as soon as we can. It shouldn't be too late, but then we're young and can party all night, right?"

"Okay," Retta said and nodded, knowing full well she wasn't going to party all night. She and her aunt had a business to run the next day. She peeped sideways at Denison. So he was another one of the migratory song birds who came to Nashville for a season and when the bread played out, they went on back home to work in the oil fields, the factories or farms. At least she could put the 'rejected' stamp on him right now. Even if Retta didn't know about his Darling Emma, she didn't date, much less get serious about anyone who wanted a music career.

She wasn't afraid to live in poverty while they climbed the ladder, but rather she'd realized years and years ago that stardom was not what she wanted out of life. The money, the glory, the diamonds—all of it was fool's gold in Retta King's eyes. And although there were those dear, dear friends of her families who'd made it to the top and remained common people, there were those who made it to the top and their egos destroyed everything they had. Retta wasn't about to take that kind of chance.

"Hey, are you kin to Bill Anderson?" A young girl grabbed Denison's arm and spun him around. He smiled brightly at the girl and she all but swooned, melting in a raging teenage puddle right there at his boot tips? *And that's exactly what I do not want.* Retta reaffirmed her position as she pocketed the key and waved to Lila who was talking to an older couple.

She opened the door to a big two-story home not far from Music Row and flipped on the light switch, lighting up a lovely living room furnished with antique furniture. The dining room table was shoved against the east wall in front of a cold, natural stone fireplace, decorated with Christmas greenery and red-velvet bows. Retta smiled, thinking about the pink, black and red checks she and her aunt frantically prepared earlier today.

Retta barely had time to remove her jacket and find the matches to begin lighting what really did seem like eight million candles when the caterers arrived, and then the quiet was gone. She lit candles while they joked, talked, and set trays of finger foods and punch bowls of eggnog around an ice sculpture of a Christmas sleigh filled with gifts. There was enough food to feed Sherman's march to the sea and eggnog and punch to fill an Olympic-sized swimming pool.

Lila inherited a lot of money when she was twenty-one and didn't have to be standing out in the cold tonight yelling "Howddddy!" to everyone who came by. But Lila had been bitten by the bug years and years ago and even her money couldn't buy her a recording contract when she didn't have as much singing talent as a tongue-tied crow. Lila did the gigs out by the Opry and lived on the fringes of stardom in the evenings after she put in a lot of daylight hours running a very successful business she inherited along with the money from her grandfather.

His name is Denison, she thought as she took care of her job and blanked out the noise surrounding her. Well, that was certainly more than she needed to know, even if she was honest and admitted that there was a strong physical attraction between them. But then, why shouldn't there be? She was his opposite. Blond hair and blue eyes next to hair the color of a moonless night and eyes so deep green it was eerie. Opposites were supposed to attract and that was a fact. Besides, she would probably never see him again. When he used up all his one hundred dollar bills sending flowers back to his sweetheart in Claremore, Oklahoma, and when he figured out it took more than good looks to make it in the stiff competition in Nashville, he'd go back home to Emma. He and Emma would make a whole farm full of beautiful babies with his eyes and hair and someday he'd entertain them with stories about how he really did meet Charley

Pride when he was impersonating Bill Anderson in a gig at the Grand Ole Opry.

Retta would tell her grandchildren, if she ever had any, about the time a tall, dark stranger rode up in a big white pick-up truck to her aunt's flower shop and sent a dozen roses to the love of his life. She'd make up a whole tale about how he could hardly bear to be away from his darling and in time went back home to her to live happily ever after. A single little tear found its way to the end of her lashes and her chin quivered slightly because deep in Retta King's lonely heart she knew she'd never get a dozen roses and a card like that.

Chapter Two

"**S**o hello again, Miss Anna's Florals." Denison was right at her elbow. How in the world did he get through the front door without her even seeing him? He'd changed from the Bill Anderson suit back into his tight jeans and had taken his coat off to reveal a white western-cut shirt which looked like it just came from the cleaners. If she laid her face on his chest she was sure she'd feel a medium starch job, but then Retta wasn't about to get that close to Denison whatever-his-last-name-was.

"I'm not Anna. That's my great aunt. She owns the florist shop and I just work for her during busy times. Usually in the winter months," Retta said.

"Well, what is your name? I was so busy I didn't catch what Lila said. Was it Rita?"

"Hey, Denison, I haven't got to talk to you yet. How's Martha? And how in the world did you get her

to agree to let you come to Nashville?" Lila hugged
him like a long, lost relative. "Oh, hi Retta." She
smiled. "Thanks for opening up the house for me. I
didn't have time to really introduce you to my cousin.
He's a cousin of a cousin. Kind of a relative who's
not a relative. Anyway, our families have known each
other for years. He's from northern Oklahoma. A little
bitty place right outside McAlester. That's down south
of Tulsa. Remember when we were kids and I used to
tell you about going to the farm and how bored I got?
Denison Adams meet Retta King."

Martha, Retta thought. *He sends flowers to Emma
and Martha isn't supposed to let him out of her sight.
Maybe Martha is the wife and Emma the darling.* Further proof that she surely didn't want to get to know
this cowboy one bit better than just his name.

"So your name is Retta," he drawled when Lila was
called away by another friend to meet someone else.
"Is that as in the feminine form of Rhett as in Rhett
Butler of *Gone With the Wind*?"

"No," she shook her head. "It's as in the backside
of Low-Retta as in Loretta Lynn of Butcher Holler."

"Oh, so are you a singer?"

"Not in your wildest dreams," she shook her head
emphatically.

"Can't sing?"

"Oh, she can sing all right. Most of us would give
our eye teeth for a tenth of her talent. She's had the
gift since birth but it's not her bag." Lila passed

through the conversation on the way to the kitchen. "Tell Martha she owes me a phone call when you talk to her and tell her to tell the kids hi for me."

Retta set her jaw in a firm line. She shouldn't even be talking to this man. He was definitely married. He probably had a lady on the side in Claremore who his wife knew nothing about, and children to boot. He just stood there smiling down at her as if he were as innocent as a newborn baby lamb.

"So what do you do when you're not working for Anna's Florals? You can sing, but you don't. Why?"

"Because I don't want to sing. I never did. My parents wanted me to be the next superstar, so we had a deal. I would take voice lessons once a week if Daddy would let me learn to fly the King's Star," she said, then wondered why in the world she was even carrying on a conversation with this philandering fool.

"Who's the King's Star? Something to do with Elvis?" he asked, reluctant to let her get away from his side, yet feeling a strange vibe radiating from her as if she disapproved of something he did.

"It's my airplane," she snapped, her blue eyes narrowing. "My name is King . . . Patsy Loretta King. King is my Daddy's name. Patsy is for none other than Miss Cline herself and you know the Loretta part. The King's Star is a 1959 Cessna 172."

"O . . . kay," he drew out. "So you fly an airplane. You don't look big enough to be a pilot," he said teasingly.

"Oh, but I am," she said. "Now if you'll excuse me, I've got to tell Lila goodbye and go home."

"Which is where?" he asked.

"Nashville, where else?" she snipped.

"Could I call you sometime?" he asked, ignoring her barb.

"I don't think so," she said from over her shoulder as she walked away from him. How dare he think she was just another Emma, standing in line to be his woman away from Oklahoma. So he had a wife close to McAlester, and yes, she knew where that was since she'd flown all over that part of the state when she took her training. And then there was Emma in Claremore, and if she just batted her eyelashes right, she could be Retta in Nashville. Maybe there was already a Katy in Arkansas and a Sally in Kansas. Who knew and who cared?

"Hey, what did I do wrong?" he called out from across the room.

"Everything and besides you didn't do anything right," she told him as she picked up her jacket on the way out the front door, and waved goodbye to Lila.

Aunt Anna had a pot of strong, black coffee brewing in the back room when she got to work the next day. "Good morning," she called out. "Hang up your coat, put on your smock and come help me. We've already got eight last-minute orders to be delivered after you have some coffee and a doughnut or two."

"How about half a dozen?" Retta asked. "I'm so hungry I could almost eat that last red poinsettia. I bet if we dressed it up with a psychedelic bow and some of that wild purple paper, it would walk out of here by closing time."

"Honey, in a get up like that it probably would have the power to walk by itself. Nope, we'll trust tradition and if it doesn't sell we'll put barbecue sauce on it and serve it up for tomorrow's dinner," Anna said with a laugh. "How was the party? Was Brett there?"

"No, he was busy ushering the late show at the Ray Stephens, and then he was going home for the rest of the holidays. Besides I told you . . ."

"I know, I know." She laughed. "Well, that rose in the bud vase over there has your name on it. Some fellow called it in this morning and said he wanted it to be ready when you got to work." Anna nodded toward a red rose.

"Brett?" Retta smiled and tore open the card to find a note. *What is right? Denison Adams,* written in her aunt's perfect handwriting.

"What's this mean?" Retta frowned, looking up at her aunt's smile wrinkling the corners of her eyes.

"I was about to ask you the same thing. Who is Denison Adams, why is he sending you flowers, and what in the world does he mean by that message? You have a lot of explaining to do, girl. So pour yourself some coffee, grab the red ribbon and make me five

bud vase bows while you talk and eat your doughnuts."

Retta filled her in on the good looking man who
bought the flowers for his girlfriend in Claremore, who
had a wife and kids in a little town down by Mc-
Alester, and who made a pass at her at the party. She
didn't know why he sent her a rose because she'd been
as cold as ice to him and didn't even give him a glimmer of hope when he asked if he could call her later
in the week. Besides he was another one of those crazy
people who thought all they had to do was open their
little mouth and a recording company would be standing beside them with a contract.

"So Denison Adams is the one who sent the flowers
to Emma yesterday?" Anna tried to put it all in the
proper perspective. "And Lila said he had a wife
named Martha and some kids? It's strange that he
would send you a rose, knowing that you knew all
that, isn't it?"

"Some men have egos bigger than their belt buckles
and an inflated idea of their own worth." Retta giggled. "Crazy man. It would take more than a rose in
a vase to make me hand over my phone number. I
wonder what Emma gave him to get a dozen roses."

There was a mad rush in the middle of the morning
and then business began to dwindle as people realized
that even the last minute had escaped. It was Christmas Eve and if the presents weren't under the tree by
mid-afternoon it was too late to worry about it. Anna

made a pot of apricot tea and brought out a foil wrapped loaf of her own special pound cake.

Retta asked, "Is that what I think it is?" Her eyes lit up. "Do you think we should save it for tomorrow's dinner?"

"Nope, got other plans for dinner tomorrow," Anna's blue eyes twinkled in a bed of wrinkles. "We've worked hard and made it through one more Christmas season. Old Santy Claus himself hasn't worked a whit harder than we have. So we're havin' pound cake and tea, shutting down an hour early, and treatin' ourselves to long, hot baths. Then tomorrow mornin' bright and early I expect you to be at my house for gifts and breakfast. And then there's a surprise for Christmas dinner."

"Yes, ma'am." Retta watched her slice healthy chunks of pound cake and lay it gently on paper towels. "Any woman who'd argue with that kind of plan would have grits for brains."

Anna smiled.

A few bashful snowflakes fell on them as they locked the door to Miss Anna's Florals. The sky was gray with no breaks so there would be more aggressive ones joining their shy cousins before long or Anna King wasn't nearly the weatherman she claimed to be. "White Christmas after all." She pointed to the sky. "Give me a hug Retta and go soak for a long time in a nice warm bath."

Retta fought a lump in her throat when she hugged

her great aunt—the only family-member she had left outside a few cousins on her mother's side in Arkansas. But she didn't really know them. They were only names in the Christmas card book and they sent a wreath to her parent's funeral, but none of them made an appearance. But then, why should they? Ruth Mason King was the oldest of four children, but the three younger siblings were born to her mother and stepfather. Ruth's father died when she was a year old and she was fourteen when her mother remarried and started another family. The half-siblings were only babies when Ruth went to Tennessee to work and she met Bob King.

"See you in the morning," Retta whispered to her aunt.

"Hey Retta," someone yelled from the parking lot.

"Looks like Lila's here," Anna caught a snowflake on her tongue just before she opened the door to her car. "Don't stay out too late and oversleep." She wagged her finger at Retta. "But don't pass up a good time either. Tell Brett or Denison or whomever takes your fancy tonight hello from your old auntie."

Retta frowned at her, narrowing her eyes and pursing her full mouth into a firm line of aggravation. The tender moment passed along with the lump in her throat. Aunt Anna knew how to rile her!

"Retta," Lila called again and waved from the car door. "Come here," she yelled.

Retta's 1984 Chevrolet truck was parked right next

to Lila's Cadillac, so she was heading Lila's way, but she'd be hung from the nearest oak tree with a brand new rope before she let Lila talk her into a party this evening. She wasn't putting herself in the position to bump shoulders with Denison Adams again. He made her heart do too many flip-flops and she'd vowed long ago she wouldn't even give a man a second look if he had country music notes floating around in his eyes.

"Hi Lila." She leaned slightly and propped her elbows on the edge of the car door.

"Well hello again." Denison said from the passenger's seat, leaning down to see her better.

She wanted to spout off a long string of words unfit for mixed company, but she bit her tongue. Evidently just merely thinking about the good-looking, green-eyed, dark-haired devil had the power to produce him in living Technicolor. There he sat in Lila's car like some kind of wealthy king being transported around by a female chauffeur. Really, now, he should be in the back seat and Lila should be wearing one of those funny little caps.

"Cat got your tongue?" Lila asked with a grin, watching the sparks fly and hoping they didn't set her aflame in the crossfire.

"No," Retta said and flashed her best fake smile. "Just tired."

"Well, crawl your happy self in the back seat and let's go to my house. We're having a private party tonight. Samuel is coming over and his sister and her husband. Denison is a third wheel or is it a fifth wheel?" She laughed at her own joke.

"No thanks." Retta shook her head.

"Why? You shouldn't spend Christmas Eve alone," Denison said. He winked at her but it didn't produce the smile he'd hoped for.

"How I spend Christmas Eve isn't one bit of your concern," she said emphatically. "Merry Christmas Lila. I'll bring your gift over tomorrow evening and we'll exchange like we always do."

"You're being rude," Lila whispered out of the corner of her mouth. "Denison isn't the plague."

"Isn't he?" Retta whispered back. "See you later," she said aloud.

By the time she walked around the back of Lila's car going toward her own truck, Denison had opened the door and was in front of her. She had to go over him or through him because there certainly wasn't room to go around him. The brooding look in his eyes said volumes without a word and the way he crinkled up his chin when he bit his lower lip would look almighty good on a Country Music Television video. It would probably make all the little girls and even a few grown women just melt in their boots, but all it did was set a flame to Retta's anger.

"Did you get the rose?" he asked.

"Yes. Thank you," she answered; her big blue eyes locked with his as the snow began to fill the inches between them. She wondered, as the heat from their gaze filled the small space, how the delicate snow-flakes survived. They should be melting and landing on the pavement in warm raindrops.

"So what is right? I'd like to know," he asked.

"Search your own heart," she said flippantly, taking a step forward but he didn't back up.

"What's that supposed to mean?" he asked. He wondered why he was wasting his time with this short blond who evidently wasn't as taken with him as he was with her. He couldn't remember the last time a woman treated him like a bag of dirt. He was the most eligible bachelor in the whole county back in Oklahoma and Lila said her friend, Retta, wasn't married, engaged or even seeing anyone. So why was she treating him like this?

"No riddles intended, Mr. Adams," she smarted. "Now if you'll move, I've got to go home. I'm tired. I want a long hot bath and a nice quiet evening and you can go to your party and learn how to be a fifth wheel. Or if that doesn't suit you, Lila knows lots of single women you can flash your pretty smile. Some who don't even care what you left behind."

"What'd I leave behind?" His eyes widened. "What-ever are you talking about, Retta?"

"Don't you play some innocent knight-in-shining armor with me." She took another step forward and they were nose to nose. She could smell the wonderful woodsy aftershave he wore. She could see the tiny yellow flecks in his mossy green eyes. [Even if you weren't married and even if you didn't have another woman on the side.] Remember I'm the one who ordered the flowers for Darling Emma with a capital D. Even if you had a gajillion dollars, an oil well in your back yard and a fleet of airplanes with your company name on the side, I wouldn't go out with you, Denison, or even play sixth wheel so you didn't feel left out. I made a vow when I was a teenager that I wasn't getting tangled up in country music. Not singing it. Not standing on the sidelines for a man who sings it. None of it. I don't want one bit of it. So put that in your little pipe and smoke it." She pushed him out of her way and hurriedly crawled into her truck.

"Wait a minute," he said with a chuckle, knocking on the window. "You got things all wrong. Besides even up on that soap box you're ranting from, you didn't tell me what is right."

"Well, right ain't you honey." Retta shook her head and gunned the motor, laying down a healthy ten feet of tire rubber on the concrete parking lot as she sped away. "Wrong?" she muttered. "I don't have things wrong, Denison Adams. You do. And I'm going to give Lila a piece of my mind tomorrow that will make her ears burn for a week. How dare she ask me to even out the numbers at her little private party with a married man."

The red light flashed on her answering machine when she walked in the door. It was too early for crop dusting so no one would call about that. It was too wet for a fire so she didn't need to take the King's Star up to fire bomb. She'd just left Aunt Anna and she was fine. Then that little voice inside her heart started battling with her. Even though she didn't want to talk to Lila or her cousin from Oklahoma she did need to push the button. What if Aunt Anna had a wreck on the way home? What if she was laying in a hospital and needed her?

She threw her purse on the sofa in the living room of her tiny apartment and sighed loudly, then hit the play button. "Retta, it's Auntie. The whole town is dead so I'm already home, but I just realized I'm out of milk so could you pick up a gallon for me tomorrow morning if you can find a place open. Love you swee-tie."

Retta peeled out of her coat and pitched it toward her purse. "Merry Christmas, darling." She recognized Brett's voice. "Been forever since I've seen you. How about dinner next week when I get home from the folks. We're doing the traditional dinner thing tomor-row. Just finished gifts with all the cousins, nieces, and nephews. Didn't know I had so many relatives. Be glad to share them with you any time you give up that stupid childish vow you made. I'm going to make it big someday and I'd love to have you on my right arm when I do. Have a wonderful day tomorrow and give Auntie my greetings."

She shook her head and unlaced her shoes. "Retta,

what in the world is the matter with you? I've seen you in some powerful snits but this one takes the cake," Lila scolded. "I'm not explaining the whole situation on an answering machine. You know how I hate to talk to them. But tomorrow we're having a visit and you're going to listen to me for a change. Leave your ear plugs at home."

"Oh sure," Retta giggled. "I'll bet I listen to you, Lila."

She ran a bubble bath, wishing for the deep claw-footed tub in the house where she grew up. Now that was a real bath. Gallons and gallons of hot, steamy water and bubbles all the way up to her chin. They didn't make tubs like that anymore—at least not in one bedroom apartments.

She sunk down as far as possible, stretched all five feet two inches out until her toes hit the end of the tub, and tilted her head back to rest on the narrow ledge. The hot water eased the ache from her legs and feet but it didn't do a thing for the one in her heart. She hated Christmas last year and it didn't look like it was going to be any better this year. Auntie did what she could to make it special but it wasn't the same since her folks had died.

After the bubbles went flat and the water fast approaching the cold stage, she hopped out onto the bath mat, wrapped a towel around her body when the phone rang. She checked the ID thing her aunt insisted she have. "You never know what pervert might be calling.

Only answer the numbers you know," she'd said when she ordered the service for Retta.

It was Lila's number. "She can call all night," she muttered on the seventh ring. "I may have to listen to her tomorrow but tonight is mine. So Merry Christmas to me," she said, but the ache in her soul was still there.

Chapter Three

"Get four plates," Anna told Retta. "We've got company coming for Christmas dinner."

Retta nodded. Last year she and Anna had eaten alone in quietness, but that was a year ago, and Auntie told her again this morning it was time to let wounds heal and to stop mourning for her parents and get on with life. But it was a lot easier said than done since somewhere down deep in her heart, Retta still felt guilty for not giving country music a half-hearted try. Her parents really wanted her to sing and she should have done it for them. But now it was too late.

"Who did you invite? Your Sunday school buddies?" Retta twirled the red linen napkins into the bright, polished silver napkin rings shaped like jingle bells. "Or have you got a couple of handsome old gray-haired fellows vying for your attention."

"It's a surprise." Anna grinned, her eyes glittering

31

in a bed of soft wrinkles. "And I'll have you know young lady, I might be seventy-five-years-old but that don't mean I couldn't steal the heart of a man who's still got black hair. I'm not relegated to the back burner with only bald headed or gray-haired men with dentures." She wagged a finger under Retta's nose. "Now light the candles so they'll have some wax on the sides before our guests arrive, and from the smell of it, that bread is about finished, so you can take it out of the oven."

"Smells wonderful, Auntie." Retta patted her affectionately on the shoulder. "Nothing, absolutely nothing smells as wonderful as the aroma of fresh baking bread. It's my favorite thing about Christmas."

"Oh, and I thought it was all those packages you tore into." Anna rolled her clear blue eyes. "Or the pound cake. Or maybe the turkey and cornbread dressing. . . ."

"Oh, hush." Retta giggled, enjoying the light hearted feeling surrounding her. It was almost as good as the last time she awoke in the old farm house outside of town to a blustery Christmas morning when her folks were still living. She'd thrown on a tattered old chenille robe and eased down the stairs to find her mother already cooking dinner, and her father wrapping the last present.

Retta hugged the memory to her heart. It was the first one she'd produced in a long while that didn't bring tears to her eyes. Maybe the healing process was beginning. "So do I get clues," she opened the oven, a rush of heat flushing her face, as she took a pan of Auntie's homemade hot rolls out and set them on a cast iron trivet to cool.

"About what? How to take bread out of the oven?" Anna asked innocently.

"You know what? Who's your new boyfriend coming to dinner? Has he got kids you'll have to finish raising or is he just a leftover no one wants?" Retta pushed an errant strand of blond hair behind her ear and put a hand on her hip.

"Wait and see," Anna said sweetly. "I'm glad you dressed up a little bit. Not that you don't look just fine in jeans and a sweatshirt, but we all used to dress for Christmas dinner and I'm glad you felt like it this year."

"Me too, Auntie," Retta said softly, smoothing the front of her electric blue sheath dress down the front. "Maybe I'd better put on my shoes before your boyfriend rings the door bell. Wouldn't want him to think I was born in a barn, now would we?" Retta giggled.

She slipped her tiny feet into a pair of blue, kid-leather, flat-soled shoes which matched her dress perfectly, and toyed with the gold chain around her neck. It held a diamond drop inside an open star. It was what she found in the package her father had been wrapping the last Christmas morning they had together. "Had it made just for you," he said a bit sheepishly when she opened it. "You'll always be our star, Patsy Loretta," he used her whole name like he'd always done. "I couldn't catch a real falling star for you, but when you look at this you'll know that I would if I could."

The doorbell rang just as she finished lighting the last red taper in a perfectly straight row of six strung down the long dining room table. Aunt Anna had inherited the house from her parents and it looked the same way it did the whole time Retta was growing up. She stopped and gave a little prayer of thanksgiving for that. At least, even in the face of disaster, there was something to hold on to.

"Come right in here," Anna's voice held excitement when she opened the door. "Just look how big those snowflakes are. Goodness me, Lila, you didn't tell me this cousin of yours was so tall or good-looking. Now, you two get right in here and take those coats off. Lila you know where to put them. Dinner's just about ready. Retta, honey, come and see who's come to dinner."

Retta didn't have to turn around to feel his presence but she did have to do battle with her heart. It told her to run away as fast as her legs would carry her. Away from the stability she'd just been appreciating and giving thanks for. Away from the crazy feeling which made her feel like a teenager when she was in Denison's presence, and away from even her very best friend. But that would embarrass Auntie and she couldn't do that.

She turned slowly and smiled, hoping that none of

them would realize it was totally fake and pasted on like clown's make-up. "What a surprise," she murmured. "I was expecting Auntie's Sunday school buddies."

"Well, Auntie called yesterday morning and asked me to dinner since I'd been moaning about not having anywhere to go today, and I wrangled an invitation for Denison." Lila grinned. "He'd planned to eat a frozen turkey dinner in front of the television and I told him he'd be missing out on the best cooking in all of Tennessee. I didn't have to twist your arm very hard did I, sweetheart?" She looped her arm through his and led him to the parlor where Auntie had a roaring fire going in the old stone fireplace.

"No, ma'am," he said but his eyes were on the beautiful woman in front of him. At the same time his heart was doing doubletime, his mind was reminding him that she was a spit fire who wouldn't even be compatible with the angel Gabriel, himself. There were dozens and dozens of women in Oklahoma who would gladly date him, so why on earth did this piece of sassy baggage appeal to him? And besides, Lila didn't mention that Retta was going to be at the Christmas dinner. She just said that an elderly friend of hers was cooking.

Oh, well, he thought mournfully, *by the time the day is finished, I'll probably have all visions of that woman washed forever from my mind. She acts like I'm some kind of cross between a rattlesnake and a two-horned viper. After we spend the whole day together, there may not be anything left of either of us but a greasy spot in the floor where we beat each other graveyard dead.*

"So we meet again," Retta said through her slightly clenched teeth. "Did Lila tell you where you were going or is this a surprise to you also?"

"Surprise." He warmed his hands by the fire.

"Dinner is ready," Anna called. "Retta you sit here on my right hand and Lila, you sit on my left. Denison, you take the head of the table and you can say grace for us," she said with authority.

"So, now tell me all about yourself," Auntie said as she carved the turkey and helped plates. "Lila tells me you're from a little town over by McAlester, Oklahoma."

"Yes, ma'am." Denison eyed the perfectly browned turkey and appreciated the man-size helping of dressing Miss Anna loaded on his plate. This was surely better than any frozen dinner. The aroma of fresh baked bread when he walked in the door brought memories of Martha and previous holidays when she made meals like this with real bread and pies. He wondered if there would be a pecan pie hiding in the kitchen, or maybe a deep-dish cobbler of some kind.

"What little town in Oklahoma and are you really here to make a career out of music?" Anna pressed gently.

"Little tiny place on the lake called Bugtussle and

yes, ma'am, I am trying to write songs or even sing a little bit." He shoveled a fork full of the best cornbread dressing he'd ever eaten in his mouth. He rolled his eyes in pure ecstasy and moaned. "Miss Anna, this is the best dressing this side of the Pearly Gates?"

Anna chuckled somewhere down deep in her chest, making her shoulders wiggle and her eyes disappear in a bed of wrinkles. "Honey, the way to a man's heart might be through his stomach, but the way to a woman's heart is to compliment her on her cooking."

"Bugtussle?" Retta said with a frown on her face and incredibility written in her eyes. Surely he had to be kidding. Nobody really came from a town called Bugtussle!

"Yep, Bugtussle. Little bitty place. Couple of ranches, few houses, a Baptist church and a way to get to the lake," he said between bites.

"But isn't that where Granny Clampet is from? I thought it was make-believe," Her eyes were as round as silver dollars.

"Might be, but it's also where I'm from. Grew up there my whole life. Granny did insist I go to school in McAlester. She had Jim Bob drive me and the kids there everyday and come get us until I got old enough to drive, then I had to take all of us. I'd rather taken a hungry billy goat most of the time than take the kids, but Granny said they'd go with me and they did. Because if Granny ain't happy then ain't nobody happy and that's a fact."

"Goes the same for Martha," Lila piped up. "She's just as bossy as Granny and she'd put you around the corner fast as Granny could."

"You got that right." Denison nodded.

"And who is Martha?" Anna asked. "Your sister or wife?"

"Oh, no," Denison almost choked on a bite of sweet-potato casserole. "Martha and Jim Bob are the help at the ranch. Jim Bob is the foreman to use the term loosely. I guess I was about five when he and Martha came to the ranch. I kept whining to Granny that I needed kids to play with and she was tired of trying to raise me and run the ranch too. Granny hired Martha as the cook and housekeeper and Jim Bob as the manager, foreman and hired help. None of the titles do either of them a bit of justice. Martha had two little boys. Thomas was four and Matt was three when they came to live with us. And we always called them the kids since that's what I was interested in the most. Martha raised me right along with the kids and Granny was their grandmother too. It's like we're family but not blood," he tried to explain a connection deeper than mere words could ever make clear.

"I see." Anna winked at Retta who blushed.

Well, there's still Darling Emma, she argued with herself. *And besides he's still in the music business, so there.*

"The kids are both married now and each have a daughter," Lila said. "Guess we should really stop calling them the kids, shouldn't we sweetie?" She patted Denison on the shoulder.

Looks like Lila is interested in more than a cousin relationship, Retta thought. *Matter of fact, it looks like she could wrap her arms around his neck and kiss him soundly right now. Well, she can sure have him! I'll even polish one of Auntie's antique silver platters for her to carry his heart around on, because I surely do not want anything to do with him, even if he isn't married to Martha.*

"Thomas is an engineer and Matthew is a professor at the University of Arkansas." Denison looked at Anna as he continued to enjoy his dinner. "They'll be home today for the holiday."

"Why aren't you?" Anna asked.

"I was there at Thanksgiving and I'm usually gone for Christmas. Ever since I was a little kid I spent the Christmas holiday in Claremore," he said, hoping they would decide to talk about someone else for a while. All this attention was suddenly making him nervous, and when he glanced over at Retta, it was as if she could care less. He was most likely boring the girl plumb to tears. She'd made it clear she didn't even know he was coming to dinner, so she would probably rather he ate his dinner, complimented the cook, and went on his merry way.

"Claremore is Retta's favorite place in the whole wide world," Anna said. "Isn't it?"

Retta nodded.

"Why?" Denison asked.

"It's where she went to flying school a few years ago," Anna said. "Her daddy and momma wanted her to sing country music but she wouldn't do it, not even if it harelipped the governor of the great state of Tennessee. Ever since she was a little girl all she ever wanted to do was sit in the cockpit of that airplane of her daddy's. Many a time they found her asleep in the shade of the wings. So they finally gave up making a big star out of her and sent her over to Claremore to that flying school and made a pilot out of her."

"I see." Denison glanced up into the biggest, bluest eyes and felt like he could get lost in them. "The King's Star, I believe you said?"

"That's the name of the plane." Anna nodded vigorously. "If they couldn't have a star one way then I guess they'd have one by hook or crook. Retta loves the stars, don't you?"

"Oh, Auntie, Denison doesn't want to hear about my love of stars. Let the poor guy eat his dinner before it gets cold," Retta said softly.

"You haven't lost your touch." Lila buttered a second hot roll and popped a piece in her mouth. "I'd walk a mile in a blizzard in my bare feet and without a coat to get to a pan of these rolls. I love Martha's bread and Emma's isn't bad but these are scrumptious."

"Emma?" Anna's quick mind picked up on the lady who got a dozen roses. "Is that your special lady?"

"She's special." Denison laughed out loud. "She's my other grandmother and she usually claims me for Christmas. She's my mother's mother and as eccentric as they make them. We never knew if she was going to be an Indian in full regalia or dressed like Marilyn Monroe complete with wig and red dress. She insisted from the time I could talk that I call her Darling Emma. She wasn't about to be old enough to be a grandmother, she said. I practically had to promise her the moon and stars and the person who made them to stay in Nashville for the holidays. You would have thought I'd broken one of the commandments."

"Oh, your grandmother," Anna shot a sly look at Retta who had another bout of high color in her cheeks. "So you sent her all those roses to make it up to her that you wouldn't be there?"

"Yes, ma'am and I may have to walk on hot coals yet." He chuckled again.

Where's your mother and father? And why do you talk about your grandparents and the hired help but not your parents? And why do I care anyway? The questions bombarded Retta's mind as she kept shoveling food into her mouth so she'd have an excuse not to ask or answer questions.

Late that night Retta laced her hands behind her head and stared at the ceiling. There was no doubt that she was attracted to that tall, good-looking Denison Adams. Everything about him appealed to her. He was from Oklahoma. He lived on a ranch and he was so handsome it took her breath away. If it hadn't been for that folly about being a country music star she might even give Lila a run for her money with the fellow. But like Auntie always said, "No ifs, buts or maybes."

They'd played Monopoly and Auntie, bless her match-making heart, tried all afternoon to throw them together in one way or the other. Tomorrow Retta promised herself she would have a long talk with her aunt while they cleaned the shop. It was traditional to clean the place on the day after Christmas. Business was nonexistent but it was a good time to take stock of ribbons, supplies and get the place back in order. They'd have a few weeks of normal breathing space and then Valentine's business would hit like an atomic bomb and before five o'clock on February 14th, the place would literally look like a tornado and a hurricane had a boxing match in the middle of it. Then Retta would have to make a big decision. Would she take the King's Star on the run this year or stay in Nashville and help Auntie?

She tossed the idea around for a while. The money was fantastic. Crop dusting from south Texas all the way to the Canadian border. A week here, two weeks there, and a few days north until the crops were harvested. The plane was in good repair and could do the work and who knew, somewhere in the middle of Oklahoma she might meet her knight-in-shining armor. The one who was going to ride up on a white horse and ride off into the sunset with her—and who couldn't carry a tune in a bucket with a lid on it.

And yet, Auntie wasn't a young chicken anymore, and Retta could make enough money to survive with her localized crop dusting and fire bombing. She might not have a nest egg at the end of the fall, but she wouldn't starve. After the dinner she'd consumed that day and the supper Auntie forced on them all before they left, she could do with a few days of starvation. She smiled at the thought.

"And I don't need to think about Denison. Lila wasn't even subtle about the way she was slapping her brand on him. Cousins or not, she's . . ." she was talking aloud to herself when the phone rang. She fumbled across the bed to the nightstand and groped until she picked it up on the third ring.

"Well, what do you think?" Lila giggled.

"About what?" Retta asked. "I loved the bracelet you gave me. Thanks again."

"That's not what I mean and you know it, Retta King," Lila scolded. "What do you think of Denison?"

"He's all right, I guess," Retta said. "Guess you found out he's more than just a cousin."

"Oh, no," Lila snorted something between a gasp and a giggle. "Denison is like a big brother to me. Now if Thomas was still available I might like to date him. You ain't never seen good-looking honey, until you see Thomas. He's something to behold. But, Denison? I don't think so. Besides he's not my type. I like the tall, blond Greek god look. And besides, guess what I just got for Christmas?"

"Did Samuel bring you a present?" Retta held her breath.

"Yep, guess what?"

"Come on Lila," Retta begged. "You know I'm horrible at guessing games."

"The biggest diamond ring you've ever seen, and he even got down on his knees and did the whole nine yards. He's sitting right here and we're planning a summer wedding. Will you be my maid of honor?"

Retta squealed in delight. Samuel was a pediatrician and he and Lila had been dating for months. "I'd love to. Just don't make me wear yellow. I look awful in yellow." She laughed.

"Wouldn't dream of it, darlin'," Lila said. "It'll be electric blue and ecru. Denison really was impressed with you and Auntie." She changed the subject abruptly.

"I'm not interested," Retta said tightly. "He's here for the music and you know my vow on that."

"Yep, I do. Just remember what Grandpa used to tell us when we were just teen-agers. What will be will be in spite of what you vow. And what ain't to be might be anyway, so put that in your brain and think on it. I've got to go now. Samuel and I are going over to his parents to break the news," Lila said.

"Congratulations, Lila. I'm really glad for you," Retta said honestly.

She'd read the situation wrong after all, she thought as she put the phone receiver back in the cradle. She was happy for her dear friend and she'd be in a whirlwind of parties and wedding preparations for the next few months. She'd be needed in Nashville to stand beside Lila through the engagement. The decision was made in that instant. She would not go on the crop-dusting run.

"There goes the knight-in-shining-armor for this year," she sighed as she shut her eyes tightly. But all she saw was mossy green eyes gleaming at her over the Monopoly game.

Chapter Four

Retta slipped into a basic black dress. The same one she wore the last three years to Lila's New Year's Eve party. Each year she swore she'd find something to wear and each year when the day arrived she wanted to kick herself firmly for not shopping. At least it was made of that slinky material which was never out of date and she could roll it up, throw it on the floor, run over it with a truck, let a family of cats sleep on it for a month, or pack it in a suitcase and it still looked like it just came off the rack at the store.

"Well, what do I do to it this year so everyone won't think it's the same one I've worn for the last three years," she muttered as she slipped it up over her hips and reached around her back to zip it, struggling to get the zipper high enough so she could catch it by readjusting her arms over her shoulders. "Might be worth being married to a country music star just to have someone handy to zip my dress," she mumbled with a smile on her face.

She'd worn red shoes and accessories last year, so that was out even if her red shoes were the most comfortable for dancing. She opened the jewelry box on her dresser and the gold star caught her eye. That's what she'd do this year—gold star, gold stud earrings and simple black shoes. No glitz or glitter. Besides Lila and Samuel would be the king and queen of the holiday with their newly announced engagement.

Brett would be there. He'd left another message on her machine while she was at work today. And so would Denison—Lila had already told her that bit of information. Well, she could give them both the cold shoulder. She'd had lots of experience these past months with Brett already. Even if she wasn't attracted to him, at least she knew how to avoid his advances. She could easily transfer the same tactics to Denison if she needed to. She probably didn't have a thing to worry about. Denison would be the eligible bachelor of the evening and all the single women would flock to him. He'd be so busy he wouldn't even know there was a short blond in a dress she'd worn three years in a row in the room with him. There would be plenty of females with the same stars in their eyes as he had, and they could stand in the corner and talk contracts, demo tapes, and back-up singers to their heart's content.

She pulled her blond hair up into a twist and held

it fast with a gold clip. The simplicity of the black dress accented her pale, flawless complexion, making her classic, timeless beauty look like it was carved from porcelain. She grabbed her jacket as she passed the sofa in the living room. The worn, soft brown leather was the exact opposite to her long, slim evening gown with its slit up the side to midway between her knee and hip, but Retta had no intentions of buying an evening jacket. New Year's Eve at Lila's was the only time she even wore the black dress. Sometimes she did dress up for church on Sunday morning or Christmas dinner at Auntie's. But an evening coat or even a dress coat—she shook her head just thinking about it. She couldn't justify the expense, even if Auntie and Lila both fussed every time she put the leather jacket on with a fancy outfit.

She locked her door and watched her step down the slippery stairs to her little blue truck. Parked right beside it was a big, white truck. A grin tickled the corners of her mouth as she lifted her dress to keep it out of the slushy mud. Maybe the knight-in-shining armor who was supposed to be somewhere in north Texas or anywhere in Oklahoma had heard her moan when she made the decision to stay in Nashville rather than going on the crop dusting run. Perhaps his heart was already attached to hers and he knew that she wasn't going to come hunting for him, so he'd come to Tennessee to find her. He'd rented an apartment in the same complex she lived in and one day she'd open her door and there he would stand.

"When pigs fly," she told her overactive, vivid imagination as she hopped up into her truck and slammed the door.

Denison crossed his arms across his muscular chest and listened with one ear to a story an aspiring singer was telling him about a contract. So this was the Nashville scene he'd wondered about all his life. The one Norman, his friend in college, salivated about when he picked up his guitar every evening. Norman said he'd make it big someday and his name would be in glitter and lights. He'd come back to Oklahoma in a flurry of fame and they'd probably even name a street in Haileyville after him.

He'd been in Nashville six years and so far there wasn't a street with his name on the sign and from what he'd seen in Norman's apartment he sure wasn't wallowing in glitter and glory.

"And then the man said, 'Honey, do you know how distinctively different your voice is? I think we might have a star here,' and I about fainted on the floor right there in front of him," the girl said with a broad wink to Denison. He smiled at the right place and remembered how often he'd heard a familiar version of the same story from Norman. Always right on the fringes of a big company deal but never really getting there.

"Hey, man, I've got a three-month job driving a

truck for a friend, you want to come out and take over my apartment? You could step into my gig at the Opry and try your hand at a little writing or singing. You always said you'd like that," Norman said a month ago when Denison talked to him.

"I don't think so," Denison said with a laugh. "That's just a pipe dream."

But his grandmother, Gem, overheard bits of the conversation and informed him he'd worked too hard and long and deserved a bit of a vacation. Nashville would be the very thing to get him away from Bugtussle, the normal everyday routine of ranching, and what a lark it would be. He could do the gig at the Opry for Norman and play around with Lila in the big city.

"Well, did you sign anything yet?" someone asked the red-haired girl who'd been so close to a contract she could taste it.

"No, but I'm this close," she snapped her fingers and edged closer to Denison.

"That close is a mile away," a tall, blond-haired man chuckled. "I've been that close so many times it's unreal. But never let it be said old Brett doesn't keep right on trying. Someday I'm having the whole ball of wax. A tour bus with my name in giant letters on the side and a fan club with enough members to repopulate Dallas, Texas."

Denison saw her slip inside the door and berated himself for even caring. Lila said she'd be at the party but she was always late and never stayed very long after midnight. She'd also told him again that Retta had made a vow when she was younger that she'd never get entangled with anyone interested in country music. Well, he wasn't really interested. Only playing at the business for the fun of it for a few months while his friend, Norman, was off making enough money to keep him riding the fantasy trip of stardom. From what Denison had already seen the competition was stiff enough that poor old Norman might be living in illusion until he was old and gray.

"Well, here's the beauty," Brett waved at Retta and she smiled, wrenching Denison's heart and making him so angry he could have chewed up fence posts and spit out toothpicks.

"Hi, darling," Brett crossed the room, meeting her in the middle and kissing her lightly on the cheek. "You're beautiful. Marry me. We'll run off to the J.P. right now," he whispered in her ear and she giggled, shaking her head.

"And you're incorrigible," she said loud enough for everyone in the group with Denison to hear. "The answer is still no, and will be no when this century is finished and the next one is on it's way out."

"Can't blame a man for trying. Someday I might succeed." He grinned.

She didn't answer. A misty fog erased everyone in the room except Denison Adams standing against the wall with his arms crossed over his chest like some kind of Italian god. She shut her eyes, thinking that she could erase the vision, but it didn't work. When she opened her eyes the fog was gone, everyone was talking at once, and Denison was still staring at her intently. Well, he could stare until his hair turned gray and his bones turned brittle and she wouldn't care.

"Dance with me." She put her arm on Brett's shoulder.

"Sure." He slipped one arm around her waist and picked up her hand in his other one. "I wanted a wife, but I guess I can survive with a dance," he said.

Denison tried to analyze the flutter in his heart in the midst of all the noise and confusion of a New Year's party. Loud music, louder conversation, good food, and Retta looking up into the eyes of another man. What did it matter anyway? In the week he'd known the woman she'd never given him one minute's hope that she'd even consider getting to know him better. So why did he have this crazy, mixed-up feeling in his heart like he was a sophomore in high school?

She looked up at Brett and saw through the good-looking exterior to the selfish man inside. It wouldn't matter if Brett was a corporate lawyer or a professor at the university, she still wouldn't consider a long-term relationship with him. No, it wasn't just the country music thing with Brett, it was the man, himself. A dancing partner for right now, yes. A friend, maybe. A boyfriend, no. A husband, a definite, absolute never.

"Mind if I cut in?" Denison tapped Brett on the shoulder.

"Of course, I mind," Brett said, "but I'm a gentleman so I'll let you." He grinned. "Just remember, she's bull-headed, stubborn and doesn't back up an inch. And she steps on your toes if you don't go slow."

"I do not." Retta slapped his chest playfully. "I could out dance you any day of the week and you know it."

"Honey, you might out sing me and when you come to your senses you'll know that with your connections and voice, you'll have what we all want so bad we can taste it. But you could never out dance me." He chuckled as he handed her over to Denison.

"So hello." Denison slipped his arm around her waist, only slightly amazed at the electricity filling his body at just the touch of her.

"Hello," she said, deliberately flat and emotionless. But that tall, handsome cowboy from Oklahoma would never know how much effort it took to keep the lilt from her voice and the sparkle out of her eyes. Especially when he picked up her hand and she fought back a gasp as the sparks flew.

"Who is the man you were dancing with? And what did he ask you that the answer was so emphatically a no?" Denison swept her around the room expertly in a two-step that had everyone in the room forming a circle and watching them.

"His name is Brett. He asked me to marry him like

he does everytime I see him," she whispered, aware of the audience.

"So why is the answer no?" Denison asked.

"Because he's a country music wanna-be just like you. And the answer will be no until eternity," she said firmly, keeping step and enjoying the dance so much she hated to see it end.

"I see." Denison nodded seriously. Someday when he was bent with age he would look back on this experience and remember the gorgeous blond-haired lady who stole his heart the first time he saw her behind the counter at the flower shop. And even though he'd think of her fondly and the sensations she evoked in his heart, he would know he'd made the right decision the night he danced with her at Lila's New Year's party. When he found the woman he intended to spend the rest of his life with, it would be one who accepted him as is. Whether he was a country singer, rancher, ditch-digger or like his mother and father, eccentric people who chased every rainbow that popped up in the sky after a rain. As much as it was Retta's criteria that the man of her dreams not be a country singer, it was Denison's rule that the woman of his dreams would always accept him and not want to change a thing about him.

"So how's the airplane?" He changed the subject.

She cocked her head to one side, looking up at him from under dark lashes which didn't match her hair or look like they had a ton of make-up on them, either. "How did you know about my plane?"

"You told me. The King's Star. A Cessna 172, I think you said," he said. "I still don't think you're big enough to fly."

"What does it take to fly an airplane? 200 pounds of male?" she asked acidly.

"I guess not. Just that Jim Bob flies our ranch plane and I suppose I always thought about him when I thought of pilots," he admitted. "Never did really like to fly. I drive when I can. But sometimes it's necessary. Jim Bob uses the plane for crop dusting and fire bombing and even hauling us around on short hauls for sales and such."

"I see," she said. "Why do you call him both names, Jim Bob?"

"Because my grandmother is Gem and when Jim Bob came to the ranch it was confusing. So even though all us kids called her Granny, we used both of Jim's names to avoid the mix-ups. Ever do any dusting in your plane?" He kept holding her when the song ended and another started immediately. The circle around them clapped loudly and Denison nodded in appreciation. Then the people began filling the dance floor again and Denison and Retta were lost in the crowd.

"Yes, I could have gone on the dusting run from south Texas all the way to Canada this year. Did it one year, but Auntie needs me and Lila's got a wedding to plan, and I can make enough to survive around here," she said.

"Fire bombing?" he asked.

"A little. I'm not real comfortable flying in fire, but I can do it," she said, confusion filling her heart. She was supposed to hate this egotistical, overbearing man, not have a conversation with him. And she was surely not supposed to be enjoying every minute of the dance or the visiting.

"Well, I wouldn't be comfortable either." He laughed, his deep voice sending a chill down her back bone and creating a whole bevy of goose bumps on her bare arms and shoulders. No one had ever made her feel like this and he had to be in Nashville to sing. Wasn't that diabolically opposing forces at work?

"Jim Bob asked me to go with him a couple of times when the volunteer fire department in the area needed our help. I told him I'd help on the ground. Dig ditches, drive the truck. Whatever it took, as long as I had a foot on the ground," he said.

"Why don't you like to fly?" she asked and wondered where the question came from.

"My folks fly everywhere," he said. "I was born in Africa while they were in their safari stage. Taking pictures of all the wild animals and living in tents with mosquito netting. Mom has a pretty good-sized plane and whatever fantasy takes her whim she's off to see it. But I was a bit of a problem. Babies and eccentricity make strange bed partners. Nannies are hard to find who are willing to go to the bush country in Australia or to India. Besides Granny almost had a heart attack every time they took me to one of those 'forsaken' places as she called them. So finally she told them that they could live their lives anyway they wanted, but I was having roots. Dad protested a little, but Mom thought she was right, so I went to live with her when I was about three and have been there ever since," Denison said.

"You ever see them?" She couldn't believe parents would leave their child and fly off to chase fluttering butterflies, or lions, or anything else for that matter.

"Oh, sure," he laughed. "They didn't abandon me on the door step. They'd fly in and out of the ranch every two or three months, bringing me a toy when I was little or a stack of pictures to look at when I was older . . ." the song ended in the middle of his sentence and he kept her hand in his, leading her to a secluded table in the corner. "They even took me on one of their trips when I graduated. Offered to let me travel with them from then on since I didn't need a nanny anymore." He pulled a chair out for her and reluctantly let go of her hand. "But after a month, my roots needed to be watered and the ranch was the only thing which would satisfy me. I was just downright home-sick, so I went back to Bugtussle and enrolled in college. Been there ever since except for a few vacations along the way."

She nodded, biting her tongue to keep from asking

any more questions. It would be so easy to fall into a trap of her own making and wind up going back on her iron-clad rule about music people. But Retta King was stubborn and hard just like Brett said. . . . And in spite of the fact she could have listened to that deep voice tell her everything about his entire life, she wasn't going to ask another question.

"So what about you? Whatever made you a crop duster?" he asked after a minute of comfortable silence. Most women prattled on and on, scarcely letting him get a word in edgewise, but not Retta. Too bad she was so blasted stubborn.

"Airplanes," she smiled and then wiped it away instantly. "I've loved them forever. Daddy flew in Vietnam. A Cessna. In and out rescuing men, running in more ammo, whatever it took. Came home and bought one just like he flew over there. Momma moved to Nashville from Arkansas and they met, got married and had me. I grew up inside the plane and loved every minute of it," she said, looking around for Lila so she could make an excuse to leave the table.

"Then it's your Dad's plane?" Denison asked.

"It's mine now. My folks were killed in an automobile crash two years ago," she said. "They left me the plane and my truck. Taxes and bills got the rest."

"I'm so sorry." He shook his head. "Mercy, my folks are crazy as they come but I can't imagine not having them. It must have been tough."

"Still is," she said, fighting back tears. "Some days

worse than others. Auntie and I manage though and we're getting better every day."

"That's good," he said and that strange comfortable silence enveloped them again as they watched the people talking in groups, dancing, gossiping, and laughing. Both of them grateful for the calm little table for two in the back corner. Calm, collected and yet any minute anything could happen.

Retta felt like she was sitting on a keg of dynamite. Any minute Denison was going to start talking about how close to a contract he was getting, how he'd actually met the Opry stars and they were going to help him get on an inside track, how he'd sang on the strip and he just knew one of the men listening to him so intently was interested in making him the next superstar. Denison wallowed in the compatible silence, wishing for what was not even remotely possible. He found himself wondering what exactly he was doing in Nashville, Tennessee. Like he told Retta earlier, his roots were needing a drink of water and the only place he wanted to drink from was the well at the ranch.

"Okay, okay," Lila yelled above the noise and confusion. "It's count down time so you'd better find someone. Ten, nine, eight . . ." she watched the clock and counted slowly, letting several seconds tick off between her words.

Retta stood up with the intentions of excusing herself and hiding out in the bathroom like she did every year. ". . . seven, six . . ." Lila giggled when Samuel hugged her tightly.

Denison met her as she rounded the table, going in the direction of the staircase. He touched her shoulder gently and even though the New Year's kiss might be the only one he ever got from Retta he intended to have that much for future memories. He gazed down into her big, blue eyes as Lila smiled from across the room "five, four, three, two, one," she said all in one breath and the clock bonged twelve times.

Time stood still for Retta and Denison as the catering crew tossed confetti and streamers from the second floor balcony. She couldn't make herself blink and look away from those dark green eyes.

When his lips met hers she thought she heard bells ringing, but surely it was just all the New Year's noise. He was twenty-eight-years-old and had kissed many women in his lifetime but, nothing prepared either of them for the sensations flowing through that kiss . . . or for the realization that even though the attraction was intense and each of their souls craved the other for completion, it could never be. It would always just be a star that fell one night and burned out on the way to earth.

Chapter Five

Retta put the *Floyd Cramer* CD in the player and leaned back in her father's old, worn tan leather recliner. Surprisingly, for the middle of winter and between the Christmas holiday and Valentine's day which were usually slower than molasses in December, it had been a hectic two weeks at the shop and her feet hurt that evening when she got home. She shut her eyes and tried to block out the ever-present vision of Denison Adams. She hadn't seen him since Lila's party when he gave her the kiss which nearly knocked her socks off. Evidently it hadn't affected him the way it did her, because he hadn't called, sent another bud vase with a rose or anything else.

And that was good!

If it had made his skin tingle like it did hers, all his good senses would fly right out the nearest window, his brain would go into reverse, and he would have

61

been on the phone twenty minutes after she left the party. But there were lots of pretty women in Nashville wanting the same things Denison did and Retta had made it clear from the very first she was not interested and never would be. Maybe one of those beautiful, future singers would steal his handsome heart away and they could even win the next Country Music Association award for duet of the year.

Come to think of it, she hadn't even heard Denison sing. She'd seen him in the Bill Anderson suit at the Opry a few weeks before, but the other times she'd been around him he'd worn typical western wear. Perhaps he had a fabulous ability and he had the looks to go with it, or maybe with all his wealthy, eccentric parent's connections he had a foot in the door already. She turned the CD player off and turned on the television, half expecting to see him in a brand new video on the Country Music Television station.

"Well, drat it all anyway," she fussed at herself. "This is the craziest thing I've ever had to deal with. I'm not going to love him, like him, or even care about him. It's simply mind over matter. I can and will deal with my fluttering heart and my stupid brain. I can and I will." She slapped the throw pillow with force but it didn't make her feel any better. "Besides he doesn't feel the same way I do—thank goodness for that much!" She hopped up from the recliner and went to the window to watch the snowflakes float down from the sky. No stars tonight. Only a dim grey layer of clouds with no personality or style.

Denison finished the gig at the Opry and drove back to Norman's apartment. Lila had been busy with her engagement plans so someone else was Minnie Pearl tonight. He sat still in his white truck listening to the end of a *Floyd Cramer* tape and watching the snow fall in huge flakes without really seeing it. He'd laughed at folks who believed in that old fantasy about love at first sight. Love was something that developed out of a friendship, something that started with a foundation and then was built a brick at a time and then blossomed into a lifetime relationship.

It was not walking into a flower shop, finding a cute little blond and suddenly his heart flopping around in his heart like it was going to break loose and dance a jig on the countertop separating him from Retta. It was not a kiss to celebrate the birth of a new century and feeling like he was standing in the middle of a meteor shower. That wasn't love! It was school-boy infatuation.

"But, what a dream," he muttered. "Too bad she didn't get struck with the same bolt. I can't imagine living like that every day. And yet, since I've felt it, I can't imagine living any other way."

He opened the door to his truck, stepped out, and looked up. Someone was in the apartment next to Norman's place. He could see the shadow behind the curtains looking out. It was a woman with her arms folded across her chest as she stood in silent repose, evidently watching the snow fall. She was about the same height as Retta but then every short woman he saw was that height. And every time he saw a blond ahead of him on the sidewalk, for just a moment he thought it might be Retta. Every time he saw a blue van, he checked the side to see if it could be the florist van making a delivery. And every time he'd been disappointed. Besides if Retta lived that close to him, Lila would have already told him.

"Where does she live?" he'd asked Lila after Retta excused herself to go to the ladies room when the new year was born. "Just tell me where she lives so I can show up on her door step or give me her phone number. I tried every R. King in the book and she's not there."

"Can't," Lila laughed breathlessly. "She'd tack my hide to the smokehouse door, and that's a fact. Just give it some time and don't be impatient, honey. You might be surprised who shows up on who's door."

"Time . . . impatient . . ." he groaned loudly. "Find someone I'd gladly fly all over the world with . . . even to Africa or India . . . just to get to be in her presence. And Lila says time and patience."

He shut the door behind him, turned on the light, and peeled out of his red Nudie jacket. This was supposed to be a fun vacation from the ranch, not a search for a soul mate and peace of mind. He started a warm shower and took off the rest of his suit, hanging it neatly in the closet with Norman's other gig outfits. It was fortunate they were the same size. He fit right into the part.

Had Norman ever met Retta? He'd certainly never mentioned her. He did talk about Lila but then Norman knew Denison and Lila were cousins. He tried to remember the women Norman did talk about. The only one he mentioned regularly was his neighbor. Some lady who brought him homemade bread and watered his plants when he was gone if he couldn't find someone to live in his apartment and help him with the rent. Probably a little gray-haired granny with an apron and a big heart who felt sorry for the young man who worked until the wee hours of the morning just trying to find a nick in the country music armor.

He wrapped a towel around his trim waist and literally fell into the bed, his head bouncing off the pillow. He laced his hands behind his head and let his mind go where it wanted—to the place he'd fought tooth, nail, hair and eyeball to keep it away from. The dark ceiling was like one of those flip-up screens his folks used to show slides of their travels. Only instead of tigers, lions, and bridges over massive gullies, it showed Retta. There she was making that bright pink ribbon bow to put around a poinsettia. So strange for the holidays and yet so elegant. And there she was standing before the fireplace at her Aunt's house on

Christmas day in that beautiful dress which made her look like a porcelain doll. Or in the black dress a few weeks ago at the party when he kissed her. Letting his mind have free rein didn't help at all, it just made his heart ache worse.

Brett waltzed into the florist shop with a big grin on his face. He didn't stop in front of the counter like a regular customer but kept on going until he was in the back room where Anna and Retta worked on a huge casket arrangement of red roses, gladiolia, and ferns. "I did it. Now will you marry me." He grabbed Retta and twirled her around the room.

"You did what? And the answer is no." Retta laughed.

"I got a recording contract. I make my first single next week, and from there it's just a hop to the moon." He laughed. "Lila says we'll have a party next week to celebrate. We could announce our engagement then and you can ride to the top of the roller coaster with me, Retta." He set her down.

"You're serious?" Anna asked.

"As a heart attack" Brett looked deep into Retta's eyes. If she said yes, he'd have it made since he got a recording contract on his own, she wouldn't feel like she'd used her contacts to get him started and she couldn't ever hold it over him that he'd ridden into stardom on her coattails. If she said yes after two years of asking, he could use her inside track to make it further and further and with a little persuasion he could convince her to sing with him. With her strong voice, he'd be assured of a place in the Country Music Hall of Fame.

"No," Retta said. "I don't love you."

"What's love got to do with it?" he asked. "We'll make the best looking couple in the whole state. And when the cameras flash, they'll see the Country Music Association awards lined up in the glassed-case in our mansion. We'll make a pair, honey," he hugged her tightly to his side. "Just open your eyes and see what everyone else already sees."

"No." She peeled herself away from his side. "I'm glad for you Brett. It's what you've lived for, breathed for, and waited for. And I'm glad for you. Get out there and knock them dead, honey. And find a woman who'll love you."

"Don't say you didn't have first chance." He warned with a shake of his finger. "I'd give you the moon, sweetheart."

"I don't want the moon," Retta said softly. *I want the stars,* she thought but she just smiled at him and went back to placing the long-stemmed roses in the casket piece.

He left, floating on a cloud of dreams, and Anna shook her head in amazement. "How could you do that? He honestly proposed to you and you turned him down. He's in love with you, Retta."

"No, Auntie. Brett will never love anyone more than

himself. The man looking back at him in the mirror is the most important person in his whole life. And if I ever got between him and that person, I'd be kicked out the door. It would only be as long as I kept him happy, sacrificed my wants and hopes and dreams for him, that he'd be happy. I'm not making much sense, Auntie, but being married to Brett is not better than being an old maid."

"I'll take your word for it," Anna sighed.

"Didn't you ever have a feller who pursued you, one who . . ." Retta tried to put frustrating feelings into words.

"Henry Haynes," Anna nodded. "He had a farm west of town fifty years ago before the town was as big as it is now. I'd just inherited the folk's house, and he had his eye on what it would bring on the market. He insisted that he loved me and I was the only woman in the whole world for him. What he really wanted was for me to move to the farm and help him raise his six kids. His wife had died having the last one a few months before and his sister was tired of the responsibility. He wanted me to give him my money, raise his kids, and make jelly. He was a good-looking man and I was already in my late twenties, an old maid in those days. But I never did like to make jelly." She cackled out loud.

Retta laughed until tears rolled down her cheeks. "Henry Haynes and Brett are cut from the same bolt of cloth. In six months he'd be trying to make me sing with him. Or make jelly and I don't like to make it either." She slapped her knee and kept laughing.

"Here we sit, making a casket piece for the preacher of one of the biggest churches in town, and we're laughing like two demented women," Anna wiped her eyes with the back of her callused hand. "What about that good-looking Denison Adams?"

The laughter stopped as suddenly as it began. "Whatever brought that up?"

"Just a thought. He looked at you like he was plumb moonstruck at Christmas? Has he called since then? I was sure you'd be going out to dinner with him or to a movie or something? Don't tell me I put on my best behavior and that boy didn't even call you. I even let him win at Monopoly."

"No he hasn't called," Retta mumbled. "And like I said all along, he isn't any more my type than Brett. I'm not making jelly for either one of them," she declared but it didn't bring back the light-hearted mood. "And you should have whipped him soundly. You never let me win anything."

Denison really had intentions of using another florist. It was just punishing himself to open the door to Miss Anna's again, but it was such a good excuse that he could even elude his own heart into believing he was just going into the shop for flowers for Martha's birthday. Retta might not even be there. She was probably out flying her little airplane around checking out the possible places for crop dusting.

He took a deep breath, took off his Stetson and opened the front door. It was too late to back out now and besides, like he'd already told himself, she wouldn't even be there. "Hello," he called when no one came to the front counter after a few moments.

"One minute," her voice came floating on the air. "Be right with you. Oh . . ." she stopped dead in her tracks when she saw him standing there, looking just like one of those men who rode horses in the cigarette ads. Marlboro was it? Whoever, there he was and she gave a sudden, silent prayer of thankfulness that Auntie was getting her hair done this morning. It was hard enough to disguise her feelings last week when Auntie brought his name up out of the clear blue.

"Hello, Retta," he said cheerfully. "I need to place an order for some flowers to be sent to Martha. Tomorrow is her birthday. What would you suggest?"

"Roses?" she said lamely.

"No, that's Darling Emma's flower. Martha likes more color. Fix me up something with lots of color, like that," he pointed to a picture of an arrangement with purple, yellow, red, and pink all intermixed together. "Kind of looks like the wildflowers she gathers every spring and puts all over the house. Wonder we don't always have a rash of chiggers the way she brings those weeds inside." He laughed but she caught the wistfulness in his voice. She'd bet her bottom dol-

these weeks so it
in anything for
He's just being
him to.

In less than fi
bag full of taco
refried beans. H
amongst green fl
and bits and pie
served, madam,"
from Taco Bell
the table from ea

"Yep, right tl
'fridge and ice i
and he went to
just hate restau
sugar," he said.
sugar you put in
let's dig in befor

"Denison," sh
lunch but I wan
right now. I enj
company and I
estly. "But that
going to let mys
ing that neon ra

"Sounds like
sexy mouth turn

lar that Denison Adams was getting homesick, just like he did back when his folks took him on a trip right after he graduated from high school. Well, if he was going to make it in show biz he'd better buck up and get over that malady. It might be months and months between visits if he ever reached the top of the success ladder and went on tour.

"Okay," she nodded. "Want to sign a card?"

"Sure," he looked at them for a long time, trying to decide on just the right one. Finally he picked out a plain card and signed, "Love, Denny," on it.

"Denny?" she asked before she thought and then berated herself for the one word question. What endearment anyone called him didn't really matter to her or did it?

"She shortens everything." He blushed. "She's always called me that. Thomas is Tommy and Matthew is often Matty. Everyone else calls us Denison, Thomas and Matthew, even Jim Bob, but not Martha." He fell into the easy conversation just like he did on New Year's.

"Oh, I see," she said. "Well, these will go out today and they'll deliver them tomorrow, then. Anything else?"

"Yes, would you go to lunch with me?" he asked in a gush before he lost his courage, knowing she was going to say 'no' as emphatically as she had told that Brett fellow no when he proposed that night. It was only a few weeks ago but somehow it seemed like a

lifetime had pas
his arms and kis

"Can't. Aunti
noon. She's got
morning, and th
have tea with he
back until three
the excuse. "Bu
from she though
some tacos we c
a whole raft of l
scheduled for to

And now I ca
at herself. *It ha*
wants, no matte

"Love to," he
whose tacos you

"The cheapest
half a dozen an
tortillas for dess
the back and cc
drinks," she sai
spend at least a
probably ask he

Oh, don't be
heart chided. *He*
probably has a
women who are
they're all busy

"I mean it," she vowed, but she wouldn't look at him. "Now, tell me how old is Martha tomorrow?"

"Who knows?" He wanted to grab her and dance around the table like a fool with cheese and lettuce stuck to his front teeth. She'd actually admitted that she enjoyed the kiss. Maybe it meant that the heaven's opened up and showed her a glimpse of a lifetime of happiness just like it did for him.

"She doesn't tell her age?" Retta smiled and her eyes actually twinkled. "I may like this woman."

"You would. When you meet Martha you'll love her. Everyone does," he said.

"When I meet her? Is she coming to Nashville? Did you get a contract?" she asked.

"Nope, and I probably won't and no, she isn't coming to Nashville, Retta," he said. "It was just a figure of speech, I guess," he wished he would have used another florist after all. Because it was as plain as the nose on his face that Retta King was never going to be anything more than a sweet memory.

Chapter Six

"Whew!" Anna wiped her forehead with the back of her hand. "I'm glad this day is finished. One more honey-sweet sentiment and I believe I'd puke."

"Auntie!" Retta shook her finger across the table. "Remember what you told me when I was a little girl. Puke is as dirty as any other four letter word. It's low-class and unlady like."

"Still is but I'd still do it if the day wasn't finished. Sometimes I hate Valentine's Day worse than any other holiday." She fanned herself with an advertisement slick. "Probably because there's not a good-looking hunk sending me flowers and candy," she smiled brightly. "Which reminds me, why didn't you get anything today? Is Brett waiting to give you a big diamond tonight? Or what about that other good-looking fellow? Denison? The one I let win at Monopoly and caught eating tacos with you a few weeks ago. Why didn't one of those fellows send you flowers or bring you a big box of candy today? Oh, I know, I know. You're not interested. Well, honey I wouldn't be either if they both forgot me on Valentine's Day, and that's a fact. Even old Henry Haynes brought me a little box of candy on Valentine's Day. Of course, I probably wouldn't have gotten it if he'd known I was going to turn down his proposal the next week." Anna laughed.

"I love you Auntie." Retta kissed her aunt's wrinkled cheek, picked up her purse, and fumbled in the side pocket for her keys. "I'll be here bright and early tomorrow morning to help clean this pig sty, but I'm not going to answer those questions. You know the answers already and I'm not rehashing it today."

"Stubbornness, pure old stubbornness," Anna huffed. "You could have your choice of any man in all of Nashville. You could be on the stage every night and have a tour bus or even a jet airplane if you'd just open your mouth and sing for these folks, but oh, no." Anna shook her finger back at Retta. "But I'm not getting into that old argument with you tonight. I don't have the energy and I would fight to the draw. I love you, too, sweetie. Go home and get some rest. I'm right behind you on my way home to prop up my tired feet and watch reruns of Matlock on television. Now there's a good-looking man."

Retta waved over her back as she shut the door. Good-looking, handsome, charismatic. They were out there by the droves. So why did one particular fellow have to haunt her dreams. She hadn't seen him since that day her aunt was talking about. It was as if the wind swept him into the flower shop that cold, blustery day when he ordered flowers for Martha. They had tacos and visited most of the afternoon and then he was gone. He didn't say he'd call her; he didn't press for another date. Apparently he wasn't as affected by her as she was by him, and even if he got a case of love-sick jitters every time he laid eyes on her, it didn't matter. There wasn't enough dirt in Texas to make her go back on her vow at this point.

She tossed her purse on the sofa beside the door in her apartment, kicked off her shoes, and melted into her recliner, the one her father had sat in all of her life. The leather was as soft as baby's skin and if she stretched her imagination just slightly she could still smell her father's aftershave when she was a little girl and curled up in his lap.

"Daddy," she murmured aloud shutting her eyes in weariness, "I'm so tired and so confused. I wish you were here to visit with me about this crazy, absurd problem with Denison Adams. I can't get him out of my mind . . ."

She opened her eyes and looked out the window just in time to see a falling star. A weak smile played at the corners of her mouth but it didn't fully materialize. Her father might be able to kick a star out of the sky to please her but he couldn't talk to her.

"Thank you, Daddy," she said aloud as if he were in the living room with her. "I love it and I get to make a wish. But what do I wish for, Daddy? Someone to take him out of my mind or the courage to go back on my word?"

Denison circled the parking lot in the apartment complex and frowned when his assigned place had a little white sports car taking up his space. Someone must have failed to tell their visitors to park in the back and not in a reserved spot. It was the first night since he'd been in Nashville that he didn't have a gig of some kind to do for Norman and he was at odds with himself. He'd already accepted the fact that he was as homesick as a six-week-old puppy who'd been taken away from his mother. He missed Granny and Martha and Jim Bob, but most of all he missed the spaciousness of country living. He longed for a lazy day on the banks of the lake with nothing but a fishing rod and reel and a tackle box, or a ride on a three-wheeler to the backside of the ranch to check on the cattle. Anything but this horrid, cramped apartment living. Not even immediate stardom with all its glory and fame could entice him to stay in Nashville one minute longer than March 15 when Norman would come back from his truck-driving stint to search for that neon rainbow, as Retta so aptly put it that day.

"Now why did I think of her?" he muttered as he climbed the stairs to his one-bedroom prison apartment. *It's because I'm lonely and homesick, and Norman or a band of angels bringing me peach cobbler on a silver platter won't persuade me to leave Oklahoma again. At least not for three whole months at a time,* he thought.

He threw his coat on the sofa beside the door and kicked off his boots. He eased into the recliner, picked up the remote control from the end table and flipped on the television. He leaned back and shut his eyes listening to an old video of Vince Gill singing "High on That Mountain." He opened his eyes just in time to see a falling star outside the window. It left the sky in a blaze of glory and burned out just beneath the window sill.

A wish, he thought lazily. *And I don't even have to fight with Thomas and Matthew about who saw it first. Now what do I wish for? An instant contract to sing in this land of stardom? No, sir! I think I'll wish for Retta King to move out of my thoughts or else change her mind about never trusting a country music wannabe.*

That brought a frown to his handsome face as he drew his heavy black eyebrows down into a straight line over those mossy green eyes which mesmerized Retta. He pushed the button, turning the television off. He went to the refrigerator in search of something to eat in his boredom. Only the curled up remains of a frozen pizza and two shriveled apples. He opened the cabinet doors. Instant oatmeal—Martha would shudder at such food. Microwave popcorn and packets of instant hot chocolate, two cans of salmon, and a dozen cans of soups of one sort or another. Perhaps he should go out and eat. He might see some of the folks he'd met at the Opry. But he didn't want to listen to talk about new songs and contracts.

However, if he stayed in the apartment another minute he was going to suffocate. He opened the door and stepped out on the landing. He drew up a green plastic chair, evidently one Norman put there for nights when he needed to sit outside and think of something new to write a country song about. He propped his sock feet on the railing and folded his arms across his broad chest. If he shut his eyes and inhaled deeply he could pretend he was just outside the cabin at the back of the property. The fireplace was roaring inside and a pot of beans were bubbling on the back of the stove. Jim Bob would be back in a few minutes from checking on those stragglers in the herd and they'd dish up the beans with big hunks of lean ham and visit about whether to sell that old Angus bull this year or keep him one more season. He did throw some fine calves but he was getting as temperamental as Granny when she didn't get her way.

He didn't even hear his neighbor's door open but he knew the instant Retta was in his presence. The perfume. The aura surrounding her. The sharp intake of breath when she saw him sitting there. His senses reeled. One wanted to know exactly what she was doing in his apartment complex. Another wanted to take her by the hand and pull her down into his lap for a long, lazy kiss. Still another wanted to simply get up and go back in the apartment and ignore the woman. All she'd ever done was throw his good intentions back in his face and tell him she wasn't one bit interested in him or his ambitions.

"What are you doing here?" she demanded. "You have no right to be sitting on my landing . . . and where are your shoes?"

"I might ask the same questions." He looked up at her. "Are you visiting Norman's little old lady neighbor who makes bread for him sometimes? Does another one of your aunts live in there?" He nodded toward the door. "Miss Anna didn't mention a sister. Or is it an aunt from the other side of the family?"

"Little old lady?" she huffed. "Is that what Norman said?"

"He said there was a little lady . . ." Denison shot right back then realized Retta was standing beside him in her socks and she didn't have a jacket on either even though it was cold in the night air. "What are you doing here, Retta?"

"I live here. Right here," she pointed toward the door with her apartment number.

"And I live right here in Norman's apartment while he's gone." Denison smiled. "Wonder how it happened we haven't run into each other before now. Amazing, we've both been up and down these steps for weeks and weeks and not once have we ever bumped into each other," he said, suddenly remembering the night he saw someone standing upstairs looking out the window at the stars when he came in late from a gig. It had been Retta. It hadn't been someone who reminded him of her, like he'd thought in the beginning. Like a hundred other women who he passed on the streets, or who came to the Opry. Like all those women who made him remember the short blond-haired lady with the prettiest blue eyes he'd ever seen, but who weren't really the right woman. "Here pull up this extra chair and have a seat. We'll visit and watch the sky to see if there are any more falling stars until we freeze."

"Did you see that star?" she asked in amazement.

"I saw one a few minutes ago. Did you see it, too? Don't tell me you saw it first. I saw it just as it cleared the top of the window, so it's my wish, Retta. I'll fight you for it," he argued like a little boy.

"I saw it just as it cleared the top of the window too. I'd fight you for it, but I think we saw it at the same time, so we each get half a wish. What'd you wish for?" She sat down with the grace of a ballerina, but her heart was doing some kind of fast-paced polka dance while her mind was running in reverse, trying to figure out a way to move in with Auntie until the day Norman came back home. To know he was somewhere in the city was one thing but to know he was right next door was more than she could even begin to think about rationally. She'd like to sit down in his lap, put her arms around his neck and lay her head on his chest to see if his heart was doing doubletime like hers. She'd like to pull his face down to hers for a long, passionate kiss that would seal their fates together forever. But she did nothing but sit down in the chair beside him.

"So what'd you wish for? A contract and a tour bus?" she asked and wondered how in the world her voice could sound so calm and nonchalant.

"Nope, you can't tell your wishes, Retta," he answered and remembered the look in Lila's eyes when he asked for Retta's address. She'd been right next door all this time. No wonder he felt like she was so close he could practically smell her perfume when he came home late at night. She'd probably been standing on the landing lots of times, leaving behind a waft of that wonderful, light scent she wore. They might be separated by only the space of a two-by-four wall stud and two sheets of sheet rock, but they'd just as well be a hundred miles apart for all the good it would do him. Next time he saw that wicked Lila he intended to give her a proper lecture.

Now he had less than a month and he'd be back on the ranch with nothing but a few memories. But it really didn't matter how long he had. He'd have no more success with Retta than if she was having tea with the queen in England and he was a pauper who collected the trash from the royal palace.

"So what are you doing out here in the cold?" Something in her mind told her to chase back in the house and start packing but her heart argued that she should visit with him a while. Her heart won the argument even though she knew she should listen to her mind.

"The apartment walls began to fall in on me. I admit it. I'm homesick. Jim Bob can take care of things better than I can, but I miss running out to the back of the ranch to check on the cows. I miss breakfast with laughter and talk around me. And I miss family."

"And what do you think is going to happen when you woo someone with your voice and tomorrow you're walking up the aisle to get a Country Music Association award for the Horizon Star?" she asked bluntly. "It'll be months and months between visits to Oklahoma. Your life won't be your own anymore. You'll belong to the fans and the agents who make arrangements for tours. You'll spend all your time working for the very thing that keeps you from going back to where you want to be."

"Do you not ever feel the magic?" he asked without answering her question. "The magic of the business. Don't you ever want to know that rush of adrenaline when you know there's a house full of people in a concert hall and they say your name and the whole place stands up as you come out from behind the curtains? Or like you say, when you've cut a couple of albums and you're nominated for a CMA award?

Don't you ever crave that camera zeroing in on your face as you smile in expectation? Or do you ever think about one of those big glass awards sitting in a big mansion. Imagine living in something other than a one-bedroom apartment? You have been here your whole life, Retta. You have got a wonderful, unique voice according to Lila and everyone else who just about swoons when your name is brought up. The magic is yours and you don't want it. You could still have all the magic if you just nodded your head."

"That isn't magic," Retta said painfully as she thought about saying almost the same words to her father the year before he died. "It isn't and it never can be." Funny, how just saying it to Denison brought a measure of peace she hadn't known when she said the same thing to her father.

"Oh?" Denison raised an eyebrow and waited.

"No, it's not magic. It's a lot of hard work, a lot of waiting, and wanting so bad you can taste it. I can appreciate those who've made it to the top and those who are still working for it. It's not that I'm putting them or their dream down. They're entitled to it if that's what they want. But, I've seen it all, Denison, and I don't want any part of it," she said again for at least one of a dozen times since she'd met him.

"Well, how in the world do you think we failed to bump into each other all these weeks?" he changed the subject abruptly, not wanting to talk about her intentions.

"Because I get up early and go to the shop and you leave before I get home. You spend half the night doing gigs and I spend all day making flowers," she said flatly. "Does Lila know you're living here?"

"Yep, and she knows where you live. I bet it's been mighty hard on her to keep that secret," Denison vowed he was going to strangle the girl until she was blue.

"Probably," Retta shivered. "I'm cold so I'm going back inside," she announced. She wanted to ask him to come inside for a cup of coffee to chase the chill away but that was asking for trouble, and no matter how much her heart yearned, she had enough stamina to overpower its crazy desires. For the first time in her life she had second thoughts about her determination to never get involved with a man with treble clefs and guitars in his eyes, yet she couldn't make herself dive into a relationship without first at least thinking about it—long and hard.

"Me, too," he agreed, thinking about asking her if she'd like some popcorn or a cup of hot chocolate. But by the set of her jaw there was no doubt she would definitely refuse. She might actually live next door, but for all the good it did him, she'd just as well live in Houston, Texas.

"And Denison, don't be fooled into thinking all this neon and possible stardom is magic. It's really not. You asked me what is magic. It's not tourist traps and wanna-be singers. Like I said that's hard work, tunnel vision, and perserverance. There's nothing magic about it. Magic is something more than can be explained. It's the tiny little green buds on a bare tree at the beginning of spring. It's a toddler when he lets go of the coffee table and takes his first wobbling steps. It's a baby bird learning to fly for the first time, or the look on a little boy's face when he hits his first home run. It's the wonder in a father's face when he looks in the nursery window at his newborn child. Or it's a falling star on a night like this. That's what magic is, Denison," she said and slowly shut the door to her apartment, leaving him on the landing still looking down at the place where she had been standing.

Chapter Seven

It was an uncommonly warm day for the end of February in Nashville. Every fiber of Retta itched to fly, but she didn't have a single reason to burn fuel. Crops weren't ready for dusting. Fire season was several months away so that was out, and even though she'd mentioned that she'd take Auntie up just for the fun of it, Anna had declined emphatically.

She wandered aimlessly around the apartment that Saturday afternoon. The shop closed at noon. Auntie went off on a sight-seeing trip with her Sunday School cronies. She'd probably seen the Belle Meade plantation a hundred times, but every time she came back from a tour she declared it was the prettiest she'd ever seen it. Maybe that's what Retta needed. A nice afternoon meandering around the grounds of an old restored plantation. One never knew, her knight-in-shining-armor might be there waiting for her to

home where he belonged and ranch the rest of his life. She could laugh and her big, blue eyes could twinkle when he told her he knew this lifestyle wasn't for him the first week he was on vacation in Nashville, but she was too stubborn to put her hand in his and trust him. So that finished that even before it got off the ground.

"Spring fever. Martha says it's when young men get an itch deep down in their hearts and can't scratch it. It's when there's not a girl in the whole county who is safe from cupid's arrows. Even the ugly ones look good when spring fever hits. And it's when old men get an itch in their overalls and want to dig up the earth and plant gardens. I guess I'm pouting. At least that's what Martha used to call it when I was a little boy and in a mood like this," he said slowly. "I talked to Thomas on the telephone this morning. He and Matthew, their wives, and daughters are driving down to Bugtussle tomorrow morning. It's Martha and Jim Bob's anniversary and Granny has a party planned. Neighbors, friends, and family and I can't go. It's an impromptu thing; Granny planned the party at the last minute for a surprise and I'm in a grand funk since I won't be there. If they'd let me know earlier I could have gotten someone to do my gig tonight and I could've flown into Tulsa and rented a car."

"Couldn't you catch a late flight and still make it. Maybe Jim Bob could pick you up," she offered.

"Nope, that would spoil the surprise," Denison said.

"I'll just have to suck it up and realize I'm a grown man and . . ."

"I'll fly you in," Retta said.

"You?" Denison said amazed that she'd consent to sit in such close quarters with him for that amount of time.

"Sure. You buy the fuel and I'll fly you over there. It should take about four hours but we could get you there by lunchtime tomorrow. Is that when they're having the party? After church? Then we could fly back in the middle of the afternoon and be back in Nashville by dark. No problem. I'm like those young men only my itch is wanting to fly and I don't have a single reason to do so."

"Are you serious?" he asked. "We've got a landing strip at the ranch. Jim Bob flies in and out on it, so you could set your plane down."

"Sure, I'm serious. Like I said, I've been itching for a reason to fly." She smiled.

"Deal," he stuck out his hand and she reached to shake with him—the mere touch of their hands making their hearts do triple time in unison.

Retta removed her hand from his and held it behind her, sure that if she looked at it, it would be fire-engine red. Probably about the same color as her cheeks at that time. She didn't intend for this to be anything but a transport service. Just a reason to fly over the countryside. So her crazy heart and soul could just stop doing the watusi and be quiet!

"What time do we leave?" he asked, a grin so big on his face she felt like he was a little boy and she'd just given him a whole sack of candy.

"Well, if you want to be there at noon, then let's see, four hours probably?" she asked businesslike.

"Eleven hours by car," he said.

"Four. Maybe five by plane. Cessna's are reliable old girls but they're not lear jets. They're slow. And we'll have to stop at the Little Rock airport to refuel so we'll need to allow a little time for that. But if we take off by seven, betcha I could have you there by noon," she said.

"You can come to the party too, and meet Jim Bob and Martha and Granny," he said excitedly.

"Oh, no," she shook her head. This wasn't going to be a *go home and meet the family* day. "I'll take a good book and a couple of bologna sandwiches in my handy-dandy little cooler and stay at the hangar. I can entertain myself for hours so you don't have to take me to the party. They'll be excited to see you and it's Martha and Jim Bob's day, so I'll fly you in and back out but I don't intend to go any further than the strip."

"Okay," he said but determined that once he had her on the ranch, he'd make her change her mind. Or Granny would when she came down from the house to pick him up. He'd call her right now, this minute, and tell her he was flying in for the affair and all about Retta. He might even admit his attraction for the lady and then Granny would move Heaven and sell shares for oceanfront property in the Sahara Desert to get to know her better.

"It's high time you found a wife," Granny kept saying these past two years.

"But Granny," he always moaned. "It's not like buying a heifer or a new hat. One doesn't just go out and find one they like and write a check."

"Nope, they don't. But they don't find one spending every waking minute on this ranch either. If you don't socialize a little more, you're going to be an old bachelor so set in his ways no one will have you, Denison. You're looking thirty right in the eye and there's lots of good women right here in this county. But since none of them can get you to take them out more than one time, I think you should go to Nashville like Norman said and let Lila introduce you to her friends." She drew her dark green eyes down until she peeked out at him through mere slits.

"Lila's friends are all sparkle and fool's gold. Just like she is. Just because it glitters doesn't mean it's the real stuff," he snorted.

"Oh, hush," Granny said. "You just go find a nice woman and bring her back here to the ranch. I'd like to see a great grandson before I die."

"You'd sure be welcome." Denison realized Retta was looking at him with a quizzical look in her blue eyes. "I was thinking about a conversation I had with Granny before I left. She insisted I come to Nashville just to see what I could do." He blushed. "There'll be lots of people besides family there. Neighbors. Everyone from the Bugtussle Baptist Church. You certainly wouldn't be intruding. And besides Granny would whip me if I left you out there in a plane with just a book and a sandwich. That's just not Okie hospitality."

"I'll fly you on one condition. You let me fly in, stay in the plane and then fly you back here. And that's the way it is or the way it ain't," she protested, her eyes snapping and leaving no room for argument.

"Then I guess that's the way it is," he nodded, agreeing with her for the time being at least. "I'll be ready at seven o'clock sharp, Captain King," he saluted her sharply, clicking the heels of his boots together, deciding on the spur of the minute he wasn't calling his grandmother and telling her anything. He'd use the three wheeler they kept at the hangar to ride up to the house on, and instead of just Martha and Jim Bob, he would surprise the whole bunch of them.

"Six-thirty. It'll take half an hour to drive to the place where I keep the plane and make sure everything is ready to fly," she told him.

"Ohhh," he moaned. "Four hours of sleep. I got the Opry to do tonight. But I can sleep on the way, huh?"

"If you trust my flying, you can sleep the whole way. You can even snore and I won't care." She smiled, just glad for a reason to crawl into the King's Star and feel the magic of flying for the first time in four months. And that was another thing to add to her list of magic things—the thrill of flying.

*   *   *

Excitement still fluttered around her at bedtime. She opted not to call Auntie and tell her she was taking the plane up the next day. After all, it was just for a day and she'd be home before dark tomorrow evening. She'd be back in the shop bright and early Monday morning when the plant salesman arrived for his weekly visit. If she told Auntie she was flying Denison home then there would be at least half-a-day's worth of questions to answer when she got back. And that would be the smallest scenario she could conjure up. The biggest one would be Auntie ordering all red silk roses and ivy for wedding bouquets while visions of long, white flowing gowns and fluffy veils danced in her head. She'd be looking at baby names and talking about getting the wooden cradle from the attic, and Retta would have to break her heart to get her off the ecstatic roller coaster of imagination.

Retta took a long bath, staying in the water until all the bubbles were flat and her toes resembled prunes. She wrapped herself in the floor length white terry robe Auntie gave her for Christmas and picked up a book to read until she fell asleep. But after she'd read four pages she laid it aside because she didn't know a single thing she'd read. She opened the doors of her closet and picked out a pair of jeans and an electric blue sweater to wear tomorrow. She laid them gently over the back of the chair beside her desk. The blue sweater matched the velvet in the chair perfectly. It had been Retta's favorite color since she was a child. The color of the stripe on the outside of the King's Star. Bright, electric blue on a white plane.

The carpet was a lighter variation of the same color and the quilt which served as a bedspread was one her mother made years ago. It was something she called a lone star quilt, done in shades of blues with lots of yellow incorporated. The throw pillows were the same yellow as a falling star and a huge oil painting of a midnight sky with the moon and stars hung above her bed. There was a single shooting star dropping from the top of the painting to the bottom, a blaze of glory. It had been a gift from her father, celebrating the day she finished flying school and came back home to Nashville. She sighed but it didn't produce a stream of tears when she thought of him like it had in the past. She took another pair of jeans from a hanger and chose a bright red sweater to take along. She packed them, along with a change of underwear, a toothbrush, hair brush, and her make-up kit inside a light weight duffel bag.

It was something she always did and seldom needed. She knew the very day she quit packing extra clothing would be the very day she dropped a chocolate milkshake in her lap or a cup of coffee on her shirt. That done, she picked up her book again, but didn't get past the first paragraph before her mind began to stray toward the things she needed to remember. Check fuel tank and make sure it was full and

would make it all the way to Little Rock. Put in the
chart bag in case she needed to file an IFR if the
weather turned ugly. She laughed aloud, remembering
the first time she asked her father what IFR stood for.
She must have been in elementary school and he said
with a twinkle in his own bright blue eyes, "It stands
for I Follow Roads. When we fly way up there and
loose our way we just get out the IFR charts and follow the roads like anyone else traveling." It wasn't
until she was a couple of years older that she learned
he was teasing and IFR really meant instrument flight
rules used when the weather was too bad for visual
flying.

She turned on the television to the *Weather Chan-
nel*. A little scattered rain to the south and clear
weather where they would be flying. She wouldn't
need the instrument flight rules or the charts. With the
kind of weather the forecaster promised she could use
her own sense of direction and VFR or visual flight
rules. A couple of hours to Little Rock, a few minutes
to refuel and grab a quick cup of coffee or a Coke,
and then on to Bugtussle. She sure hoped Denison
could find it from an aerial view, but then from the
sound of his voice he was so homesick, he could probably find Bugtussle blindfolded and standing on his
head.

She unbelted the robe and let it fall in a white puddle around her feet, pulled on a pair of white, cotton
bikini underpants and a long, flannel nightshirt which

looked like something from *The Night Before Christmas,* and tucked herself into bed, sure that she would still be counting sheep when Denison stomped up the stairs and opened the door adjacent to hers. But in just seconds after she pulled the quilt up to her chin and curled up in a ball, she was sound asleep.

Her dreams were filled with blue skies and fluffy, white clouds. Then suddenly the clouds were black and angry and she lost her bearing. There was a bell ringing, like a school bell. It seemed to be telling her to go back, not to trust her judgment in the storm and to regroup and reconsider her situation. Something was terribly wrong and she didn't know where she was or if she was right side up or upside down. Then suddenly she was in Vietnam co-piloting for her father as they flew under the dark clouds toward the river. They were flying in with a load of ammo for the troops and he was laughing, telling her not to worry. He knew exactly where he was. He could fly this old bird on fumes and a prayer. She just needed to pay attention to the controls and trust him. She awoke in a cold sweat with the covers all tumbled into the floor in a heap and her red nightshirt sticking to her body.

The phone was ringing and she grabbed for it, muttering something about it being the bell from her horrid nightmare. "Hello," she said gruffly.

"Now is that any way to treat your darlin'?" Brett asked. "Were you asleep, honey? Good grief, it's only midnight. No one sleeps at this time. It's a time to be out and playing, not sleeping. You can do that in the daylight."

"I was asleep," she told him flatly.

"Well, wake up. Put on your best jeans and your dangly silver earrings. A bunch of us are going to Southfork to dance the night away. I'll have you home right after breakfast or else I'll marry you and make an honest woman of you. And that's a promise. Pick you up in fifteen minutes?" he said.

"Sorry," she said. "I've got a job tomorrow and I'm already asleep," she mumbled, truly about half asleep, but not sorry in the least.

"I might propose to Celeste if you don't quit turning me down." He chuckled, but she could hear an edge in his voice.

"Then tell her congratulations for me," she snapped back at him.

"Retta, you're going to be sorry you didn't take me up on the proposal and sell that blasted plane. We could be really good together, honey. Both on- and off-stage," he crooned.

"Sell my plane? That's a new one, Brett," she said icily.

"Well, no wife of mine is going to fly around crop dusting and putting out fires. For crying out loud, Retta. What would the tabloids do with that? Think about the paparazzi and the headlines. Country Star Marries Common Crop Duster," he said.

"We won't have to worry about that, will we?" she

said just as testily. "It can say, Country Star Marries Beautiful Celeste in Heavenly Ceremony. Good night, Brett."

"Hey, let's don't fight," he crooned again. "Go on and do your little job tomorrow. We'll talk about our wedding seriously when you get back. I'll be able to support us both with my new contracts and you won't have to do a thing but hang on my arm and look at the camera with those big old beautiful blue eyes."

"Good night, Brett," she said again and hung up before he could say another word.

She took a quick shower to wash away the sticky sweat from the nightmare, rustled around in a dresser drawer until she found a cotton knit nightshirt with the whole Looney Tune cast of characters on the front and gathered up her quilt from the floor. She took it to the leather recliner in the living room, leaned back, and wrapped herself up. It was a safe haven and no nightmare would dare invade her dreams while she was on her father's recliner.

Chapter Eight

A soft breeze was blowing when Retta stepped out her door the next morning at exactly the same time Denison opened the door to his apartment. "Good morning, looks like old March is coming in like a lamb," he commented cheerfully. His jeans were creased perfectly, bunched up around the tops of his black eel dress boots, and his western cut shirt was the exact same color of eyes green. "Guess that means she'll go out like a lion and we'll have tornadoes to contend with at the ranch while we're trying to take care of baby calves. Could I carry that for you?"

"No, it's light, just a change of clothes in case I spill something on myself. I'm pretty clumsy," she smiled back. "Glad to see a nice clear day, though. The weatherman said there were a few scattered showers but they were south of where we'll be flying. My truck or yours?" she said leading the way down the steps. He was talking about working on the ranch by the end of the month and she was glad to hear it. Still, she had to follow her own heart's inclinations and not be a part of his life in any way, especially since he had a desire to sing. One never knew—one day he might be happy as a lark with his cows and ranch and the very next moment he might say, "I'm going back to Nashville one more time. I wrote a song out there in the back forty and I know it's a best-seller. I've got to go try."

She'd seen it a hundred times. They arrived with glittering eyes. Left when the money ran out and came back later to try again.

"Mine," he offered. "I'll drive. You can fly."

"Did you ever want to learn to fly?" she asked as he opened the door for her.

"Nope, I think I associate it with instability. At least that's what Granny says, and she's a pretty wise old bird," he answered as he drove. "Point the way. I'm really glad you're flying me today. But I have to be honest. I really don't even like to fly. Not in big planes and especially not in little ones. By the way, the invitation to join the party is still open, Retta."

"Turn left at the next light," she told him. "And thanks but no thanks. I'm looking forward to finishing a novel I've got in my bag and just sitting in the plane soaking up the aura in there. Why would you associate a plane with instability and not all this song business. It's as unstable as water?"

"Granny says the plane stuff is because of my folks," he answered honestly.

"Didn't you ever like all that travel and excitement?"

"It was all right but what I really liked was the ranch. Peacefulness, quietness, and then Martha and the kids came and it was perfect. I had someone to play with plus the stability," he said, following directions as he explained.

"Here we are," she said after a few minutes of silence. "Park right there at the end of the hangar. That's my plane right there," she pointed to a white Cessna with a bright blue stripe. "I wonder if she's missed me as much as I've missed her." She hopped out of the truck without waiting for him to open the door for her and jogged to the plane.

"If I painted a blue strip down my sides, I wonder if she'd ever be that excited to see me?" he muttered as he locked the pick-up door. "Probably not," he answered his own question.

The flight went smoothly all the way into Little Rock where Retta avoided the big airport, opting for a small one on the outskirts of town. She taxied in to the hangar so gently that she didn't even wake Denison from a sound sleep. One minute he was talking about the countryside of western Tennessee and eastern Arkansas looking like most other countrysides from the air. Except Egypt, he said. The aerial view was a big patchwork quilt, with shades of brown instead of green; all except the mountains which were showing out by with their evergreen trees before anything else could even bud out. The next minute his head slumped to his chest and his eyes were shut tight in deep sleep. Retta stole peeps at him as she flew, a peace and contentment filling her heart. When she soared above the earth even at a mere 3000 feet, she knew how the great eagles felt. How sad that anyone would ever capture one of those magnificent birds and put them in a zoo. Even the biggest aviary in the whole universe couldn't let them soar unhindered and free. Some souls weren't made to be captive. The eagles, her father's, and even hers. If she couldn't fly she'd wither up and die.

Retta brought the plane to a perfect landing just outside a familiar little airport. Bud would be surprised to see her. She hoped he was there today, but Bud was always there, breathing dust and airplanes, talking fuel and different planes. The last time she and her father flew into Little Rock, Bud was so excited he could scarcely sit still. He'd just fueled a YAK, a Chinese war plane. She and her father allowed him to show them all around the old war bird. She thought it was ugly then and hadn't changed her mind one bit since. Her little Cessna was a pretty sight like the eagles. That YAK thing reminded her more of a buzzard. But she'd done well that day and kept her opinion to herself until she and her father were back in the air.

Denison raised his head slowly, shaking the cob webs of sleep from his head. "Are we there, already?" he asked. "How long did I sleep?"

"Better part of an hour. We're in a little private airport outside of Little Rock. I don't fly this little girl into the big places unless it's an emergency. All those big planes make her nervous," Retta said. "Want a cup of coffee or a Coke? Or need to stretch your legs. This won't take long."

"I'd love to stretch out," he unbuckled his seat belt. "Coffee sounds wonderful."

Fifteen minutes later, after Retta hugged an old fellow wearing grease stained coveralls, they were back in the air. "Friend of yours?" Denison asked, sipping his coffee and admiring the way she flew the plane. A stretch limousine wouldn't have been more comfortable with the exception that he would have had a good deal more leg room.

"Daddy's," she nodded. "They flew together in Vietnam. We always fueled here when we could so they could visit. It was during one of those times I took a nap under the wings of this very airplane. Guess they lost me after a while and came looking for me. Daddy figured I'd be in the cockpit pretending to fly, but I got sleepy and the shade of the wings looked pretty cool on that hot summer day. Bud loves planes even more than Daddy and me. Oh, he says the storm the weather man talked about last night is a stinker but it's still to the south of where we'll be. Warned me to be careful, though. Guess in some places March isn't coming in like a lamb after all."

"Look up there," Denison pointed ahead to the haze obliterating the blue skies. "Your friend did say it was still south of us?"

"Yep, but it looks like it's changed course, doesn't it?" she picked up the radio and called back to Bud.

"Hey, kid," his grainy voice filled the cockpit. "You better get out your charts and file a flight plan. It's too early for tornado season but it looks like we've got a honey blowing in from south Texas. Made a left hand turn somewhere along the way and I think you're going to catch the edge of it after all."

"I didn't bring my chart bag," she moaned over the radio. "Trusted the weatherman, which is something you and Daddy have both told me a million times not to do. I can still see the ground and if it's just the edge, we'll fly through it and get on past it pretty quick. Keep me posted, Bud, if there's any change."

"Will do, Retta. You be careful, girl," Bud said.

"We can go back," Denison said. "I didn't tell anyone I was coming so they won't be disappointed. I don't want you to take chances, Retta."

"I'm not," she declared a little too quickly. "I can fly this bird upside down in the eye of a tornado," she deepened her voice and imitated her father. "Why, when I was in Vietnam I didn't even get a flight chart. They just said, fly over that river and take those troops this ammo. It was raining cats and dogs and baby elephants and visibility was almost a yard, and I got that ammo to the troops. But what they wanted worse than the ammo was the chocolate candy bars."

"Your father?" he asked.

She nodded. "The stories he used to tell kept me on the edge of my seat and begging for more. But then, you probably know as much as I do about flying even though you don't like it."

"Nope, practically nothing. I read a good book or listen to music when Jim Bob flies us to a sale or whatever. What is that about a flight plan?"

"They like us to have five miles visibility. We call that legal visibility. But sometimes in a fire it's not available. Then there is special visibility which is like the fire bombing. And marginal which is what we might be into in the edge of that storm up there. Who knows? It could make a southern turn and we'll see it off to our left dumping a monsoon season on the mountains and leaving us completely alone. I could fly north a little bit and avoid it altogether."

"Retta, girl," Bud's said again as if he was sitting on her shoulder. "The storm is wider than we figured. And longer. I think you better set down as soon as possible."

"I can still see," she said. "I think I'm just on the edge. Will call in later. Thanks, Bud," she said.

"And if it doesn't and it gets worse, Retta? What kind of visibility do you call it when you can only see a yard up ahead?" Denison asked, amazed that his

knees weren't shaking and his hair standing on end. He really didn't even like the big commercial jets, let alone these little hummers. Jim Bob could scarcely get him to go up with him and the ranch plane was at least twice as big as the King's Star.

"That's called vicious VFR," she said. "Vicious visual flight rules. And here she comes," the first drops of rain hit the windshield with force and she dropped down to 1800 feet, which was usually a great altitude for viewing farms and exclaiming about how tiny the livestock looked, but sometimes it was a lousy height to avoid TV and radio towers. Thank goodness they were in some pretty dense mountainous areas and there weren't many of those to plague her.

The first bolt of lightening shot through the air like an arrow and a prickly sensation danced up her spine. It really was time to find a place and land the plane. She couldn't see anything, not above her or ahead of her. Nothing but gray rain and lightning streaks. If she squinted hard she could almost make out trees bending with the wind and rain below her. "Time to set it down," she said calmly but Denison could hear the fear in her voice.

"How far until the end?" he asked.

"Retta, come on girl. Talk to me," Bud's voic grainy. "The storm is building power as it You've got to land. Find a pasture or a ro come back here. You'll be in the midd whole way. Can you hear me?"

"I hear you Bud," she said. "I'm hunting a site now. I will call you when we're down safe."

"There," Denison pointed to a clearing. It looked like the top of a mountain where maybe a logging crew had been cutting timber. "Is that enough room?"

"It'll have to be," she said tersely, circling three times before she finally brought the plane in for a landing. Denison held his breath and Retta fought the wind and rain with the fine-tuned expertise born of long hours of flying as she landed on the slippery black mud and slid to a stop. The nose of the plane was just inches from a huge pine tree when she brought it to a halt. Her hands were shaking and tears filled her eyes. For a split second she thought they were going to crash into the tree.

"Whew." Denison laughed nervously. "That was some fine job. I don't know how in the world we'll get it out of here, but you sure set it down in fine fashion."

"Retta, girl, are you safe?" Bud's worried voice asked.

"Safe and sound," she told him with a high-pitched nervous giggle. "Will see you later this evening for more fuel to get back to Nashville. Thanks a bunch, Bud."

Denison sighed but not audibly. There was no way he was going to make it to the party in this storm. Even if it passed in an hour, they still had the problem of getting back in the air from this unfavorable posi-

tion. *Isn't this what you've wanted ever since you laid eyes on this woman? A little time with her when she couldn't run away.*

But not this way, he thought.

Be very careful what you pray for, my son, the voice said. *Because your prayers were just answered.*

No amount of mental arguing could bring another word to surface from his heart. He had what he wanted, albeit not the way he wanted. He'd envisioned a late dinner at a steakhouse, maybe in a back corner with a red-and-white checked table cloth, dripping candles, and a slow, country two-step dance after they ate. After dancing, they'd take a ride on a river boat in the chilly moonlight, his arm draped around her shoulders and sparks flying around them like sparklers on the Fourth of July.

When Retta could breath a whole lung full of air again she remembered the nightmare she'd had last night about her father. They were flying in this kind of weather in Vietnam. And he'd told her he knew exactly where he was. He could fly this old bird on fumes and a prayer. She just needed to pay attention to the controls and trust him.

I would if you were here, she thought. *I'd sit in Denison's lap the whole way into Bugtussle and let you get me out of this mess. Mud, rain and a pine tree so big King Kong could climb it. What do I do now, Daddy?*

"Did you bring enough bologna sandwiches for me?" Denison asked.

"Sure," she nodded. "Several right in my bag. It looks like you aren't going to make it to the party on time."

A solid sheet of jagged lightning bolts lit up the sky in an array of eerie colors, illuminating deep green pine trees, dark grey skies, and pouring down rain. Before the thunder could echo the power of the lightning, a creaking noise made Denison and Retta jump and look behind them. A huge old pine tree on their right swayed in the wind, as if it was a beautiful ballerina dancing, the branches beckoning like graceful arms while the trunk worked hard to keep on its toes.

A single broken band of bright yellow reached down from the skies as they watched mesmerized, and it kissed the tree. The lightning cracked as if it had been filled with dynamite and blown apart and fell in slow motion right across the tail of the King's Star. The jolt reminded Retta of an amusement park ride where everyone screams and screams and gets off the ride with butterflies in their stomachs. She realized this was for real. It wasn't a nightmare. Her father wasn't there and the whole back end of the plane was with the trunk of a pine tree.

"Retta," Denison was screaming. "We've got to get out of here. That tree is on fire and even in the rain it's burning. We've got to get out!" He was shoving the door open and running around the plane, pushing his way between the nose of the plane and the tree in front of them. He jerked Retta's door open and took her hand. "Come on," he demanded.

"I can't leave," she said weakly. "I have to stay with her."

"It's not a ship," he said as he picked her up, noticing blood running down the side of her head onto her bright blue sweater. Tears bathed Retta's cheeks and sobs shook her shoulders. "I don't even know where to go," he said aloud as much to himself as to her. "We've got to find shelter. The lightning could strike us as quick as it did the tree."

She laid her cheek on his chest, glad for his strong arms around her, carrying her to safety. The King's Star died. There was no way King Star could ever be resurrected and Retta was numb with shock, relieved that she didn't have to walk because her knees were like jelly and her heart was broken. She raised her head to look at the plane and let out another barrage of tears. The King's Star had no dignity left. She was a mighty eagle who'd flown into a tree and the two of them toppled to the ground together. But maybe someone could make magic and put her back together again. She wasn't really dead, just injured badly. Then a flash filled the sky, it's beginning somewhere close to heaven and its point like a finger touching the tiny little airplane and instantly a loud crash surrounded the clearing. It was not as big or violent as the crash when the tree fell, but at that very moment someone pulled the life support plug and the King's Star went up in a blaze of glory. Rain fell in great sweeping sheets that should have put out any flame, and yet the little airplane continued to blaze. Wind, rain, fire, and a broken spirit all in the same moment. Retta wept.

Chapter Nine

Black mud stuck to Denison's new boots and his feet made a sucking sound he could feel but couldn't hear over the tremendous claps of thunder. The cold rain plastered his clothing to his body and chilled him to the bone. The near freezing water washed the blood away from Retta's head and he could see that it was a superficial wound. It was a hole the size of a match head and could use a butterfly strip to pull it together. When the tree fell on the back end of the plane the impact forced Retta forward and she hit her head on something in the plane. The cold rain water washed out the wound and by the time they'd walked a quarter of a mile the bleeding had almost stopped.

He could feel her sobbing against his chest but he couldn't stop in the middle of the driving storm to comfort her. He would comfort her later, if there was a later. If he didn't find shelter soon and they had to spend the night out in the elements, they'd both have pneumonia by morning. With both of them wct, hungry, and emotionally devastated it wouldn't take much to chill them to the bone. By morning, they would be delirious with fever if they didn't find some kind of shelter. Denison looked for a bull dozer or a tractor they might be able to set up camp. But there was nothing.

He'd about given up hope when he looked ahead and saw a trailer looming only a few yards ahead. "Well, hallelujah," he muttered but Retta didn't even hear him. Normally, Retta took the bull by the horns and charged full speed ahead into any situation but watching the King's Star go up in flames was more than she could bear. It was the last thing, short of the pick-up she drove, that had belonged to her parents. The house they'd lived in wasn't completely paid for so taxes and the bank took it. The plane was paid in full and she and her father had joint custody since she finished flight school in Claremore. But now it was gone too. She snuggled deeper into Denison's arms and wished she didn't ever have to open her eyes again. She was tired of cold rain, tired of hearing booms of thunder, and most of all tired of the instant replays of the streak of lightning destroying the little airplane forever.

"Thank goodness," she heard him mumble and then he set her down gently on the steps of some kind of porch. She looked around to find a tiny trailer house, one of those kind with a gooseneck which attached to the bed of a full-sized pick-up truck. What exactly was a trailer doing out in the middle of the woods on top of a mountain?

"I think it's a company office," he answered her question without her having said a word. He knocked heavily but no one answered. He tried the knob. "And the door is open. Can't get any more friendly than that." He slung the door open and hoped the wind didn't blow it shut in his face. He picked her up again as if she were a baby unable to stand on her own two legs. He kicked the door shut with the heel of his muddy boot and laid her gently down on a sofa in the tiny trailer. She shivered violently and he stood up, taking stock of the situation as he dripped puddles on the floor. A desk with a chair pushed up under it was on the end wall and a tiny kitchenette consisting of a gas stove and a little sink topped a little refrigerator, on the other side of the desk. A tiny bathroom only found in travel-trailers was at the end of a short hall. He opened doors to find a closet with blankets and a couple of shirts, a pair of coveralls, and some mismatched but clean socks on a shelf. Another door produced a fairly well-stocked cabinet of canned food, juices, coffee, peanut-butter, and crackers. At least they wouldn't die hungry.

"Okay," he went back to the sofa where Retta lay in her own puddle of cold water, staring ahead with glazed eyes. "We're safe from the storm," he said gently as he reached out to turn on the lamp on the desk but nothing happened. "Appears we're out of electricity, but there's a gas stove so we can fix food. The first thing we've got to do is get out of these wet clothes. Retta, come on." He propped her up into a sitting position.

"I can do it," she whispered. "Where's the bathroom?"

"Good girl," he praised her efforts at even talking. "I'll help you get there. There might even be enough hot water for a shower if the tank is gas powered and not electric. I found a shirt and some socks and there's even blankets and a bed up there," he pointed toward the double bed up a short ladder. "We'll have you warm in no time."

She let him support her to the bathroom and then chased him out. "I can do it by myself," she protested when he tried to bend down in the small room and help her take off her shoes. She peeled off her wet clothes slowly and found a big, fluffy bath towel in a drawer under the minuscule vanity. When she'd rubbed life back into her freezing limbs she reached a hand out the door and took the shirt and boxer shorts Denison handed her. The shorts were red-and-white striped and the shirt was a big flannel shirt in a bright red plaid which hung down past her knees. There was one orange sock and one bright green but she didn't care. To be reasonably warm and dressed in something other than soaking wet clothes made her feel almost human again. She draped her own wet clothing over the towel rack and the shower rod and opened the door to find him standing in the middle of the living area of the trailer. He wore a pair of boxer shorts with decorated Christmas trees on them and a red flannel shirt which hid all but the bottom edge of the shorts. One of his socks was yellow and the other one an argyle plaid with muted greens and blues.

"Not something I would pick out to wear to dinner," he attempted to smile, "but got to admit, they sure feel good right now. Here sit down on the sofa and I'll wrap you up." He yanked a blanket from the closet and wrapped it around her when she obeyed him without a word, tucking it in around her feet. "I found beans and soup and some coffee. No electric power. I don't know if they have a generator or some lines stretched, but whatever it is it's gone. We can boil water and make a pot of cowboy coffee if you'd like."

She nodded, and he set to work, rustling around until he had a pot of water on one burner to make coffee and another pot with chicken-noodle soup heating on the other one. "I'm sorry about your plane, Retta. You do have it insured?"

"Yes," she said, but what good was insurance. It might buy another plane. Maybe even a Cessna 172 made in the same year and she could even paint an electric blue stripe on it and name it the King's Star. No one would ever know the difference, but she would. It wouldn't smell right. It wouldn't fly the same. The door wouldn't squeak. She couldn't wiggle down into the seat and think about all the times her father had done the same thing. "Where are we? How far did we walk?"

"Not far," he said and a big blast of thunder shook the trailer, causing her to tremble and tears to sting her blue eyes as she saw raw visions of the plane on fire. "Maybe a half of a mile. Maybe even less. I hoped they'd have something up here for the lumber jacks. They usually pull a trailer in or something for an office to make coffee and keep a few records," he said, measuring coffee in the palm of his hand and shaking it into the boiling water.

He found coffee cups in the sink, rinsed out all four and poured soup into two of them. She reached for the cup when he offered it to her, sipping the hot broth and holding the plastic spoon back with her forefinger. "It's gone, Denison. My plane is gone. Just ashes and twisted metal."

"I'm sorry," he said.

"I know," she accepted his words and the tone they were offered in as honestly as they were given. "When do you think the men will come back up here?"

"Tomorrow morning." He ate the canned soup and never tasted anything so good. They were alive and had food and shelter. Tomorrow he would worry about the airplane and how to help Retta get over the terrible loss. "More? There's about ten cans in there. I'll heat another one."

"Yes," she said. "I'm so hungry. I thought we'd die.

I thought a tree would fall on us or that lightning would strike us dead," she admitted.

"Me, too," he said, opening another can of soup and pulling out the peanut-butter and crackers. He found a package of Oreo cookies hiding behind the crackers. Probably the fellow who filled out the flannel shirts should watch his calories and hid food from his fellow lumber jacks.

By the time Retta finished the second cup of soup and downed some of the stuff he called cowboy coffee, her nerves began the terrible job of untangling. Losing the plane was more than her poor heart could bear, but she was adult enough to realize that she could have died if Denison hadn't pulled her free of the plane when he did. One minute the impact threw her forward and then back against the seat, the next moment Denison was screaming while something sticky ran down her face and then he picked her up like a feather pillow and began running in the rain.

"Thank you for saving my life," she mumbled.

"Quite welcome," he wrapped himself in a second blanket. "Doesn't look like this rain is going to let up one bit, does it?" He peeped out the blinds behind the brown imitation-leather sofa just in time to catch sight of another fierce, jagged edge of light zipping through the dark sky. It was only noon and yet it was as black as midnight.

He should be walking in the door at the ranch house right now, surprising everyone, instead of sitting in a travel-trailer on top of a mountain wearing another man's clothing and looking like a circus clown. He was alive and right now that was the most important thing.

"Did you tell your aunt that you were flying me home?" he asked, hopefully.

"Nope, figured I'd be back by dark and besides. . . ." she let the sentence hang in mid air. She wasn't about to tell Denison how much her aunt teased her about him. "Did you call your Granny and tell her to put on another plate?"

"No, thought I'd surprise them all," he said woefully. "I checked while you were in the bathroom. The phone is dead." He nodded toward the desk. "Guess the storm broke down the lines. If this rain doesn't stop the lumber jacks won't be able to get up the road tomorrow. We could be stuck here for a while. Bud's the only person who knows we're flying."

"But I did tell him I'd stop in to refuel. Of course, he won't be expecting me now that he knows I landed in the storm," she said. "He'll think I waited it out, flew on in with you, and then waited to come back to Nashville until tomorrow. He might not even think about me refueling in Little Rock."

"We could be in for a long siege," Denison said. "I don't know where we are and how far we'd have to walk to get to civilization. And the storm looks like it could continue all day. Think you could sleep?"

She nodded slowly. "You?"

"I'm exhausted. I don't think even the cowboy coffee, as strong as it was, could keep me awake. You want the couch or the bed?" he asked.

"I don't want to move. Can I have one of those pillows?" she looked mournfully at the two fluffy pillows on the bed.

"Yes, ma'am. I'll throw you down one." He scrambled up the ladder and stretched his long, lanky body out on the bed. It would be tomorrow morning before Retta's aunt missed her, and tomorrow night before the Opry missed him. He vowed that when he got out of this predicament, he was making one more trip to Nashville. And that was to get his truck, his clothing, write Norman a note and stick it to the refrigerator, and go home, for good. This was enough adventure for him for an entire lifetime.

Retta shut her eyes but the pictures didn't stop. Only this time out of the wreckage, rain and smoke, she saw her father walking toward her. He had a smile on his face and a star in his hand. A real one, as if he'd reached up into the heavens and picked one out. It glistened and gleamed like real gold and he reached out to her, without a word, but the look in his eyes let her know he meant for her to take it from him. He'd finally caught a falling star and brought it to her. And the King's Star burned behind him.

"But Daddy," she said in the vision. "I let you down. Our airplane is gone."

"Oh, my child, you could never disappoint me. I

love you. Take this, study the moment, and don't lose the best star you'll ever have," he said and then a whirlwind took him away. She snapped open her eyes, expecting to see him beside her on the couch, but there was no one except Denison, sleeping soundly above her on the bed. It had been only a silly dream. She often dreamed of her father and this was just her subconscious way of dealing with the catastrophe. She shut her eyes again and all she saw was darkness as she slept the sleep only known to tired children and adults whose souls have been seared with sadness.

"What the devil?" a big booming voice blustered in the front door. Retta sat straight up, trying to collect her bearings but not doing very well at it. A headache pounded behind her eyes and when she reached up to touch her forehead she found her wound and winced. Then she remembered the wreck and the fire and why she was sleeping on the sofa in a strange trailer. The doorway was blocked with a man only slightly more narrow than the door and who was having to duck to get inside. "What are you doing in my office?" the giant boomed again.

Denison heard Jim Bob hollering at him to get up. They were in the range-line cabin where they'd been hunting deer all week and he'd overslept. He was dreaming. When he sat straight up, his head hit the top of the trailer, and he moaned as he fell back on the pillows, holding his aching head in his hands.

Since when was the top bunk that close to the ceiling? Then reality hit and he remembered where he was.

"And you, too?" the voice bellowed again. "What's going on here?"

"Just a minute man," Denison said. "I can explain."

"I hope so," the big man said. "And you better get started right now. Because I ain't got all day and if I don't like what you're sayin' then me and you and the dolly right there is goin' in to the law and let them listen to you."

"Wait a minute," Retta bounced up off the bed, flipping the blanket around her body. "You don't have any right to come in here blasting away and making threats. We've been through enough trauma these past twenty four hours to . . ."

"Spunky little lady, ain't you?" The man smiled for the first time, his blue eyes twinkling above a full red beard. "Think you can bow up to me and you no bigger than a bar of lye soap after a hard day's washin'. And wearing my shirt while you're doin' it. Okay, so don't have a heart attack, little lady. Set down there while I put on some coffee and tell me what in the world you're doin' sleepin' in my office?"

"Can't make coffee in the pot," Denison swung his legs over the edge of the bed and started down the ladder.

The man took one look at him and began to chuckle. It started as a silent heaving of the chest and turned into a full-fledged roar in seconds. "If you ain't the most pitiful looking excuse for a man I've ever seen," he wiped his eyes. "Get your clothes together and go change," he nodded toward Denison's clothing strung out all over the room. "I just got the generator back in operating order around back. We can make coffee now. And this better be a good story."

"I'm going to the bathroom and put my clothes on," Retta announced, her voice leaving no room for sass or comment.

In ten minutes Retta and Denison were sitting on opposite ends of the sofa explaining to Red Harrigan what they were doing in his office, telling him about the storm and the remains of the plane he would find in his clearing.

"And that's what happened," Denison said.

"Well, you two is some lucky kids," Red said. "Storm like that could have killed you. Glad I forgot to lock the door. Sometimes I remember when I get home that I forgot to lock it, and then I figure what the dickens. After all, it's up here in the middle of no where. Ain't nothing to rob except my coffee and crackers. Suppose I ought to take you two on back down the mountain with me. I come up here to see if the loggers could get in and it's a snap they can't. Not today anyway. They're waitin' for me to call back down at the service station on the telephone. Finish your coffee and we'll get on down the side of this messy mountain and you can call in for some help. Got relatives who can come and get you?"

"Yes, I can phone my foreman at my ranch and he'll fly over here if there's a strip where he can land," Denison said.

"Guess he could land at the hangar about twelve miles from the station. Reckon I could drive you over there once I make my calls. It's only a couple of miles off the road I'll be taking home," Red said.

"We'd be grateful," Retta barely smiled.

"You two sure you want to go back up in an airplane after what just happened?"

"Like riding a bicycle," Denison nodded. "When you fall off it you get right back on and try again."

Red took his time getting down the mountainside on a one-lane dirt road filled with potholes and as slippery as ice. It was mid-morning before he finally drove his mud splattered truck up to a small service station, grocery store, and laundromat all in one. Denison couldn't believe he'd slept from mid-afternoon, through the night in a raging storm, and until after eight o'clock the next morning. Retta couldn't believe she was sitting between two men in the cab of a dual cab truck on the way down the very mountain where the remnants of her airplane still laid in a burned heap.

"You make your call first, so your foreman can be on his way." Red motioned to the pay phone in the corner. "Can I get you something to eat?" he asked Retta.

"No, thanks. But I do need to make one phone call

when he's finished. My aunt will be worried sick," she said.

"Sure thing," Red nodded. "Hey, Buster, give me some of those Oreo cookies. Two packages of them. If I got to sit in front of the television all day I intend to have something to put in my mouth."

"Hello," Martha's voice never sounded so good as it did right then to Denison's ears. "Hello," she said a second time before he could swallow the golf ball–sized lump in his throat.

"Martha this is Denny. Could you put Jim Bob on the line?"

"Where are you?" she shouted. "We've been worried sick. Some fellow named Bud called here late last night. He said a girl he knew was flying you over here for the party yesterday and was supposed to call in when she arrived. We couldn't get hold of you and he didn't leave us a number. Lila couldn't find you and you weren't there for the show last night," she rattled on and on.

"Hold up, I'll explain it all to Jim Bob. Put him on the other phone and you can listen in," Denison said.

"I'm right here, son," Jim Bob said. "Your Granny has gone to talk to the police about a search team. I was just fixing to go up and see if I could see anything between here and Little Rock."

"We had an accident but we're fine," Denison said hurriedly. "I'll explain it all in detail when we get home. We hit the storm, lost Retta's plane and spent the night in a lumber jack's trailer. Let me put the fellow who is helping us on the line and he'll give you directions to the little airport not far from here. He's going to take us there and . . ."

"I'll be there soon as I can make it," Jim Bob said. "You can finish the story when you get here. I understand you're bringing a young lady with you. Someone named Rita?"

"Retta as in the backside of Low-retta," he said with a grin. "And yes, I'm bringing her home with me."

Chapter Ten

Jim Bob crawled out of the crimson red airplane with a white stripe down the side and grabbed Denison in a bear hug. "Son, we've been worried plumb sick. The kids are even still at the ranch. Ain't none of us slept more'n an hour all night long. Your Granny paced the floor until after midnight and then started cooking. She's made two batches of grape jelly and dozens of cookies. You know how she gets when she's nervous."

Denison grinned but Retta could see tears floating in his green eyes. "This is Retta King." Denison pulled her up to his side by wrapping an arm around her waist and she didn't flinch. "She was my pilot and did a fine job of getting us out of the storm. Lightning hit a big pine tree and it fell on the plane. Can we go home now?"

"Yes son, we can, and Miss Retta, I'm glad to make

your acquaintance," Jim Bob said as he tipped his hat toward her. "Just crawl up in one of those seats back there. Miss Retta, you want to fly this old girl home for me?" he asked.

"No, sir," she managed a weak giggle. "I'll be glad to be a passenger today."

Denison repeated the story of the accident again while they were in the air. Retta listened with one ear and tried to make sense of the crazy, mixed-up feeling in her heart. Yesterday she was dead sure she never wanted a thing to do with anyone interested in country music. But today, sitting so close to Denison Adams in the six-passenger airplane she wasn't so sure. Looking death right in the eye and coming out on the other side had altered her opinion. Somehow while she fought her heart with every fiber of her being, she'd actually fallen in love with Denison. Not with a country music wanna-be. Not with a rancher who missed his family and home. But with the man. His smile and the way his eyes twinkled when he looked at her. The way he took charge—when she would have sat in the plane a minute longer for sentimental reasons—and carried her out of danger. Even the way he put the cup of canned noodle soup in her hands, his fingertips brushing her arm and making chills the size of mountains go down her backbone. But most of all for the genuine remorse in his voice when he told her he was sorry about her airplane.

He understood how she felt. The softness in his tone

let her know he sincerely cared about how much sorrow was in her heart. She remembered her father standing there in the smoke and rain with a star in his hands. A falling star right out of the rain. What did it mean? Was it really just a mixed-up dream or did it really have something to do with Denison Adams?

Denison finished his story and the three of them flew along in silence. He wanted to reach across the arm rest and take her hand in his, but she'd probably yank it back and give him a scathing look. "How's the head?" he asked.

"Sore." She tried to smile but her chin quivered. She looked out the window at the bright, clear blue skies that were so different than the wall cloud she tangled with yesterday.

Auntie had breathed an audible sigh of relief when she heard her voice on the phone an hour ago. She'd gotten to work and figured Retta overslept so she called her apartment. When she didn't get an answer she thought Retta was already on her way to the flower shop. She got busy and an hour passed and there was no Retta. She began to worry . . . car accidents, flat tires. The phone rang and it was Bud, the man who'd served in the air force with Retta's father. He told Anna the same story he told the Adams family, and Anna's world fell out from under her. Retta was the joy of her life and to think of her laying somewhere after an airplane crash was more than she could bear.

Tears flooded Retta's blue eyes and streamed down

her cheeks, the salty taste of them even getting past her full mouth and onto her tongue, as she thought about how Auntie wept on the phone. "Oh, my child," she'd cried. "I'm so glad you're alive."

She went on to tell her that she didn't want to see her back in Nashville for a couple of days. She wanted Retta to rest and try to get over the emotional strain, and it wouldn't hurt a thing to go to a doctor either whoever Denison's grandmother recommended to get her head checked. "You never know if you have a concussion or something," she chided. "I suppose you lost your purse?"

"No, I had one of those little fanny pack things," Retta said. "With my driver's license and a credit card for gas. Didn't think I needed anything more. But here I am going to his ranch without clothes or even a tube of lipstick, Auntie," she moaned.

And if she could have seen through the lines, she would have seen her aged aunt high-fiving several stuffed animals sitting beside the front counter. Even if Retta didn't want to admit it, she was worried about her looks and that could only mean that she cared about this man she'd declared she wouldn't even look at cross eyed.

"We're home," Jim Bob brought the plane to a perfect landing. "And there's the welcoming committee." He waved to a bunch of people looking up and shading their eyes with the back of their hands.

"I look awful," Retta whispered.

"You'd look beautiful in a burlap bag with the middle cinched up with a piece of bailing wire," Denison whispered back, the warmth of his breath making a prickly sensation up and down her neck.

"Denison," his Granny hugged him when he crawled out of the plane. "That's enough scare for a lifetime. You might not be allowed to leave this ranch again until I'm dead and gone. I've never spent a worse night in my whole life."

"I'm so sorry," he apologized amidst hugs from Martha, Thomas, Matthew, and even the pseudo sisters-in-law. "I want you all to meet my pilot and my friend." He extended a hand up to Retta who waited in the plane for the first emotional onslaught to be over.

"This is Retta King," he pulled her up to his side like he did when he introduced her to Jim Bob.

"Hello, sorry I didn't get him here for the party," she said. Gem Adam's fell in love with her on the spot. The soft look in Denison's eyes said he was in love whether he knew it yet or not. This was the one. It might take longer than Gem wanted to wait for results, but Retta King was the next matriarch of Gem's Acres, and on that, she'd bet her life.

"Well, you've got him here now and we can have another party," Granny said. "Let's get in those cars over there and go home."

Home, Retta thought as she was put in the back seat of a Cadillac beside Denison. Granny sat up front with

Jim Bob driving. *Home. A place other than a one-bedroom apartment. But I've severed all the cords that might have been. I've told him repeatedly that I don't want anything to do with him since he's one of those song birds.*

"We were sleeping like hibernating bears and there's this big booming voice coming from a man bigger than Paul Bunyan filling the doorway." Denison came to the end of the story about the whole incident. Someone put another cup of hot chocolate in his hand and he sipped it, never taking his eyes off Retta, who laughed at parts of the tale and literally wept, unashamed and unabashed. She half expected him to tell the part about her father coming out of the smoke and holding out a star to her.

"Well, I'm just glad that man forgot to lock the door and that you two kids found some shelter," Granny said with a sigh. She was a couple of inches taller than Retta but probably the same size, a wizened lady without nearly enough wrinkles to testify to her age, and only a couple of wisps of gray glistening in her short dark hair. Retta could imagine her son, Denison's father, looking a lot like her because Denison did.

"And I'd have given my eye-teeth to see Denison come out of that loft-bed in mismatched socks," Thomas' wife, Ruth said with a giggle. "Denison doesn't even go to the hog lot unless his jeans are starched and ironed to perfection," she told Retta. "Stick around a few days and get to know what an old, fussy duddy he can be."

"Hush," Denison blushed. "You'll scare her away. I had to fight a storm and play a knight-in-shining armor to get her in this house." He reached across the sofa and took her hand in his, but he didn't look at her, for fear she'd be giving him a 'jump-off-the-ends-of-the earth' look.

The doorbell rang and everyone quit talking at once. "The doctor," Granny said simply. "Martha, tell him we'll be upstairs in the sitting room," she said.

"What?" Denison's eyebrows drew down in a frown.

"You've both been through a wreck and cold rain enough to give you deadly pneumonia. I've arranged for our family doctor to come out here and check you out. Both of you. Your Aunt Anna said . . ." Gem said.

"Auntie Anna?" Retta raised an eyebrow.

"Sure, we talked while I waited on Jim Bob to get you home. She called Lila and got our number and said you were stubborn as a long-toothed mule in a snow storm and probably wouldn't get that head checked." Gem motioned for a grey-haired man in black trousers and a white shirt to follow them up the stairs.

"Well," Retta snorted.

Gem said, "Sounds just like Denison." She laughed. "Sometimes you can be independent and sometimes you'll take orders. Today is order day my children. So get in there with the doc and I'll meet you in the kitchen for lunch when he's finished. The kids are going home right after we eat and then you're going to get some rest the remainder of this day." She pointed a finger and opened a door into a study.

The doctor examined Denison first, paying particularly close attention to his lungs and a bruise on the back of his neck which neither he nor Retta noticed. Retta sunk down in a leather recliner and pouted for a few minutes until she realized what she was doing and smiled in spite of the fact she really did not like to take orders from anyone. The room wasn't very big but three walls were floor to ceiling bookcases with glass doors. She saw everything from John Grisham books to those of Nathaniel Hawthorne. The other wall was solid glass overlooking the ranch. She could see a few red bud trees trying to put forth their purple flowers—the first signs of spring, the first magic.

"And now you Miss Retta," the doctor asked her to breath deeply. He checked her eyes several times to make sure she didn't have a concussion. "Lucky girl. It's just a little hole. Wouldn't have stitched it even I'd seen it yesterday and it looks like it'll heal fine. Might leave a scar 'bout the size of a green pea, but that's not a big sacrifice to pay for being alive and well today."

"Yes, sir," she said. "That bruise on Denison's neck? Is it from the whiplash when the tree hit the plane and we were thrown around?"

"I suppose, but it looks harmless enough," the doctor put his things away in a black bag. *Just like in the movies,* Retta thought.

"Thanks Doc." Denison walked him to the door. "I appreciate you taking time to drive all the way out here."

"Listen son," the doctor said and grinned impishly. "If Gem Adams ain't happy, ain't nobody happy. And I got to play golf with that woman later this week. You and your missus over there will be fine. Just rest easy today and don't go full blast the rest of the week. Young folks heal better than us old dogs, but the emotional side of a trauma like this is hard on anyone. So my prescription is that you both be lazy until Friday. Then after the weekend you can get back into the full swing of whatever you want to do. Now, I'm going downstairs and tell Gem that she can pay for the caddy when we play and you two have about fifteen minutes before she'll expect you to lunch." He winked at both of them.

"Oops," Denison said when he was out of ear shot. "Guess he thinks we're a couple."

"Guess so," Retta couldn't keep the corners of her mouth from turning up. "But if I'm a missus then what does that make you, kind sir?"

"Who knows?" Denison said with a chuckle. Would wonders never cease? She was as cold as a December frost a few days ago and now she was actually making a joke out of something as serious as a mistake like that. "Are you going to rest and recoup here at the ranch all week like he said or are you going to walk to Tulsa and catch the next flight to Nashville?"

"Is that an invitation?" She cocked her head to one side in a definite flirting manner and Denison didn't know whether to shout or go blind.

"Yes, it is." He wanted to cross the room, take her in his arms and kiss her like he did at the New Year's party, until they were both breathless.

"Then I accept. But could you possibly drive me to the nearest clothing store in Bugtussle and let me at least purchase a couple of pairs of jeans and a jacket. I don't even have a toothbrush," she moaned.

"Jim Bob will drive us both into McAlester this afternoon. I'm sure Granny won't let me drive for a couple of days. She'll be sure this bruise will cause me to have spots in front of my eyes or some other such malady." Denison felt the sparks flying across the room from the chair where she sat with her legs curled up Indian-style under her, to the winged-back chair he sat in. Twelve feet separated them, but he could feel the same tingle in his heart he felt when they sat close together on the sofa down in the den and he took a chance by reaching out to take her hand in his.

Gem sat at the head of the table for lunch. Jim Bob sat at the other end with Martha to his right. Denison was to Gem's right and Retta was told to sit right beside him. Perhaps she should tell these good people that she was just his pilot and that she'd thrown every attempt at a relationship right back in his face for more than two months. And that even though he had reached out to her a couple of times today, it was probably just a natural thing since they survived a terrible trauma together. Tomorrow he would wake up and possibly be ready for her to go away so he could get on with his life, or else he would wake up and declare they were going back to Nashville so he could be Bill Anderson in a Nudie suit at the Opry again.

She looked down the table at Thomas and his wife and their two-year-old daughter in a high-chair, across the table at Matthew and his wife, and their three-year-old daughter in a booster seat. And suddenly she knew what she wanted out of life. It didn't matter if they came here to visit occasionally or if they flew all over the world chasing lions on safaris or just looking at the Taj Mahal, or if she even relented and sang duets with Denison, she wanted him to be a part of her life, forever. But with her luck, she was probably a day late and several dollars short. Surely Denison Adams could have his pick of any of the belles in the whole state and he wouldn't be interested in a short, blond-haired Tennessee girl.

Denison snuggled down in his own king-sized bed and watched the stars twinkling in the sky from his bedroom window. Anna said Retta liked stars and she wore a diamond in the middle of a gold star around her neck. A gift from her father, he thought he remembered someone saying.

They'd shopped in McAlester that afternoon and she'd worn a lovely, flowing skirt and sweater to the dinner table that evening. She'd pulled her hair up into one of those twisted hairdos which made his hands itch to take down. It was evident Granny was quite taken with the woman and he didn't even want to hear the comments when they flew back to Nashville and he came back without her. As a matter of fact, he didn't want to think about that right now. He wanted to remember how she laughed when he had Jim Bob drive around Bugtussle and prove to her there really wasn't a shopping mall where she could purchase make-up and clothing, and how she flirted with him after the doctor left the room.

Retta pulled the sheer, white curtains back and sat on the floor crunching the thick off-white carpet between her toes as she looked out at the dark sky. Gem had insisted they retire early to rest from all they'd been through, but Retta had slept almost eighteen hours the day before and she was wide awake. She'd turned back the fluffy comforter on the bed and slipped between the sheets, but sleep would not come, no matter how tightly she shut her eyes, and so finally she pulled the curtains back and watched the stars.

"Daddy, what were you trying to give me? A star . . . but what does it mean?" she whispered. "Can't you come back one more time and tell me what you meant?"

Why should he? The sassy voice in her heart said. *Figure it out for yourself. It's right in front of your eyes and you can't see it. I know exactly what he was talking about.*

"Oh, hush," she snipped. "Whatever it meant, I know how I feel. I just wish I knew what's going on in his heart."

Chapter Eleven

The wind blows constantly in Oklahoma. A gentle breeze in the spring. Hot, blistering furnace-type blasts in the summer, cold, blue northers in the winter, and brisk winds in the fall. According to the red bud trees and tiny green color showing on the willow trees, winter was falling into the background and the gentle breezes of spring were in the air, promising pleasant days.

Retta dragged her hand in the cold water at the lake. They'd driven down a bumpy road from the ranch to a place called Juniper Point where Denison put the fishing boat in the water. They'd spent an hour watching the red-and-white bobbles on the end of their lines dance up and down in the water. Finally she gave her rod to Denison to put in a holder on the edge of the boat while she lazed back and watched the birds and clouds. It was hard to believe that just yesterday she met Granny and Martha and the family for the first time.

It was even harder to think about her airplane being gone, but somehow the aching pain wasn't there anymore. Maybe it would resurface when she got back to Nashville and the reality of what really happened finally caught up with her. She might go into a grand funk which would last for months and months, but today a peace filled her unlike any she'd known in years and years.

"Earth to Retta." Denison took both poles from their holders and put them away. "What are you thinking about?" He sat down in the hull of the boat, letting it drift on the gentle waters.

"I've got something to say and I guess I'm trying to put it into words. It's strange but I've never been at a loss for words in my life until now." She looked up at that dimple on the left side of his face and the firm, muscular lips—the ones which made her tremble a couple of months ago.

"Well, spit it out." He smiled and the dimple deepened.

"Okay, I was wrong," she admitted. "I vowed I'd never get tangled up with a country music person, and that's as far as it went. I was wrong, Denison. I forgot to look at the person and trust him. I just looked at the profession and somewhere in the course of my life, I got it in my mind that none of them could be trusted. They were out there chasing a neon rainbow with a pot of gold at the end. They'd do anything to be able to dip their hands in the pot of gold and come up with one of those funny shaped pieces of glass." She stopped and looked up into his eyes.

"And?" he asked when she stumbled for more words, his mouth just inches from hers. "Are you saying?"

"I'm saying I was dead wrong about you and I apologize for judging you," She wanted to pull his face down to hers, but he was probably fixing to chuckle and make a joke of what she just said.

"I see," he said and closed the space between them. The kiss was both gentle and passionate, all consuming and scary. It said a million words and not a one was heard outside the confines of two hearts.

"Mmmm," she sighed when he pulled away and propped himself up beside her, their shoulders touching and sparks still prancing around from the kiss. Could it be possible that all their kisses would be like that, even when they were eighty-years-old and sitting in a fishing boat like this?

"So I can call you for dinner after all? Even when you get back to Nashville?" He asked tenaciously.

"What do you mean when I get back to Nashville? I thought we both had tickets for Friday?" she asked.

"I'm only going for a day, then I'm getting in my white truck and coming home where I belong, Retta. Nashville was a lark. I write a few songs and Granny thought it would be fun for me to try my luck at selling them. But you of all people know exactly what it takes to make a songwriter in Nashville. Norman wanted me to take over his place until he got back with enough money to keep on trying to get a contract." Denison's eyes never left hers as he talked. "I found out real quick that Nashville and big city life isn't for this old country boy. Spring is coming and it's time for me to be home."

"Why didn't you tell me that in the beginning?" Her eyes flashed. How dare him lead her on the way he did. First he let her think he was engaged to Darling Emma and then that he was married to Martha and had kids, and then he didn't even tell her that he wasn't serious about Nashville at all.

"Because you didn't let me." His own eyes narrowed to little more than slits. The dimple disappeared and the cleft in his chin deepened as he set his jaw. One minute they were kissing and she was apologizing. The next they were on the verge of fighting. Was this what life would be like with Retta King? A roller coaster of passion every day?

"I didn't what?" she hissed.

"You just crawled up on that bandwagon of yours and commenced to spouting off your vows and how you wouldn't even tell me where you lived because I didn't do something right and did everything wrong," he said.

"Well . . ." she sucked up a lung full of air to continue the argument then suddenly her eyes changed and a smile tickled the corners of her mouth. He was right and she hated to lose a battle, but there was more ways to end the war than with hand grenades and army tanks. She laced her arms around his neck and brought his mouth down to hers for another searing kiss.

"I said I was sorry. Now let's fish," she murmured when she finally let him up for air. "And we'll decide what we're going to do about dinner dates later. Right now we've got about three days to see if we can stand each other or be glad to part company forever."

"Ain't likely," he chuckled and drew her to him for one more tempting kiss before he reset the poles and they began to talk about ranching and Bugtussle.

Retta called her aunt Wednesday afternoon and Anna squealed like a teenager when she heard her voice. "I'd begun to think you'd forsaken me after that short call on Monday letting me know you were alive. But not to worry, my dear. Gem and I've been talking every day. She's keeping me posted on every little thing," she crooned.

"What's that supposed to mean . . . every little thing." Retta's anger surfaced in a split second.

"Oh, like you two went shopping on Monday and you came down to supper in a lovely flowing skirt and sweater and yesterday you went fishing in one of his sweatshirts and Gem's jacket. And you were all flushed and happy looking when you came home, and for crying out loud Patsy Loretta King, if you don't wake up and smell the coffee, I may pour it on your head. Gem thinks you've hung the moon and the sun just comes out to shine on you and she says Denison is just plumb moonstruck . . ."

"Okay, okay." Retta finally giggled. "You both have stars in your eyes, and I'll have to shake them out when I get back to work next Monday. You will never guess what I'm doing right now, not in a million years."

"Looking through a *Bride's* magazine for a wedding dress? One of those big, flowing things with miles and miles of tulle . . ." Anna whispered conspiratorially.

"Heavens, no!" Retta exclaimed. "Guess again and think of the man who proposed to you. The one with all the kids."

"You're playing with a bunch of kids. Retta King, you get out in the pasture with that man and show him you're worth keeping. Don't be wasting your time with kids," Anna scolded.

"I'm not playing with kids. And Denison and Jim Bob are working cattle so they sure don't need my help this morning. Tonight we're going to some kind of pot-luck thing at the church, but right now Auntie, I am making jelly. Martha has a bunch of grape juice she canned last fall and we're making jelly. Can you believe it?"

"I'll buy a *Bride's* magazine and have it ready when you get home," Anna said seriously. "Got a customer, honey, got to run. Call me again tomorrow and I'll tell

you what I know about what you've done." She
laughed as she hung up.

After supper Retta disappeared to her room at the
top of the stairs and took a long, hot soaking bath. She
brushed her hair up into a twist like Denison liked and
applied a touch of make-up and then she pulled out
the prettiest thing she'd bought when they shopped at
a little shopping center in McAlester called Tandy
Town. It was a plain, electric-blue silk sheath with
long sleeves and a black hand crocheted sleeveless
jacket which stopped a few inches above her waist.
She couldn't bring herself to spend money on jewelry
and all her mother's things were in her apartment in
Nashville. She wore the star her father gave her and
for a minute before Denison knocked on her door, she
wondered again the meaning of the dream about her
father and the star he held in his hand.

"Well, well, well," Denison's gaze started at the tip
of her black shoes and traveled all the way up to the
top of her head. He touched the scab on her forehead,
which even make-up couldn't cover, and gave silent
thanks again that she wasn't injured worse. "Don't you
look absolutely gorgeous tonight. I'll have to super-
glue myself to your side or every young swain in all
of Bugtussle and half the county will be trying to
brand you tonight." He kissed her on the forehead and
took her hand in his. "Granny and Martha are biting
at the bit, and even poor old Jim Bob is being rushed
around, so we'd better go." He pulled her out to the

landing, keeping her hand in his all the way down the wide staircase.

"Whooo-ee," Jim Bob whistled. "You better keep latched on to her hand, son. There'll be a stampede if you ever let go."

"I intend to Jim Bob," Denison squeezed her fingers.

The fellowship hall was full and overflowing with people when they walked in and a hush fell over the entire room. "Well, well," one old fellow in bibbed overalls finally broke the silence. "Here's our boy we thought was dead and is riz up again. Kind of Biblical ain't it?" he chuckled.

"Only I wasn't dead," Denison reminded him and the talk resumed.

"Introduce me?" A young man with beautiful blond hair and deep brown eyes stepped up beside Retta and smiled brightly.

"Samuel, this is Retta King. Retta, Samuel Jacobs." Denison wanted to slap the silly look off his friend's face. There wasn't an auction block and if there was, Retta wouldn't be up for sale, and Samuel looked like he was about to bid on her anyway.

"Are you here with this scoundrel? Or could I possibly take you home tonight? I could tell you things about his wandering ways and eyes that would make you're pretty blue eyes turn brown and your hair stand on end. Let's go over in the corner and . . ." he teased.

"Thank you, but no thanks. I never go in the corner

with a man I've just met," she joked right back. "But if you two gentlemen will excuse me I'm going to the ladies' room."

She suppressed the giggle until she got into the bathroom, looked at herself in the mirror and hardly recognized the girl looking back at her. Retta King's eyes were flashing in mischief and her smile was almost infectious. She'd really thought about begging a headache and staying home tonight, but this place looked like it was going to be more fun than the biggest party in Nashville.

She opened the door to find a circle of three women standing right outside. "Excuse me," she said and started around them.

"Just a minute," a tall, red-haired woman said and grabbed her arm.

A red flag went up and Retta pulled away from the woman.

"So you're the little pilot who can't even get a plane through a little rain," the woman said acidly. "Well, I'm Terri, honey, and I want you to know Denison Adams isn't up for grabs."

"She's been seeing him for over a year," a short, dumpy brunet said bluntly. "Just go home to Nashville honey. We don't want you in Bugtussle."

"Terri, is it?" Retta said. "I'll remember that, but I don't see an engagement ring on your finger . . . honn-n-ey, and until there is I don't think Denison is branded. Have a nice evening and don't wait up for him tonight, he's got other plans," Retta said in her sweetest, southern Tennessee drawl.

"You're a cold witch," Terri said under her breath and then smiled brightly when she looked up into Denison's face. "Hello, darlin'. I was just getting acquainted with your hired help here. How about dinner at my place tomorrow night? You promised when you left at Christmas you'd bring the steaks when you got home," she purred as she plastered herself to his chest, wrapping one long arm around his neck and toying with his earlobe.

He shook himself free. "I don't think so, Terri. Retta and I are going sightseeing tomorrow and then Friday we're flying to Nashville. Come on, Retta, I want you to meet the old fellow who was teasing me." He put his arm around Retta's waist and pulled her away. "I took her to dinner one time about a year ago. She's got dollar bills in her eyes and visions of Gem's Acres belonging to her," he said quietly as they walked away.

"Oh? Well, she sure had me shaking in my boots. I was just about to tuck my tail and walk all the way back to Nashville, just to get out of her way so she could lay claim properly to you." Retta fluttered her eyelashes at him in mock seriousness.

"Oh, were you?" He raised an eyebrow and her heart fluttered.

"Yes, kind sir, I was. And I didn't know we were going sightseeing tomorrow. Martha and I were going to make bread all day while you and Jim Bob did some male things out on the back forty." She ignored the stares from the people in the room and kept up the easy banter.

"Plans have changed. Granny told me tonight I wasn't about to ignore you tomorrow like I did today. Not even if she had to hire a dozen extra hands to help Jim Bob. So name your poison and we'll sightsee tomorrow until you won't have time to sass me or make my blood boil with those sultry southern looks," he said honestly.

"That time darlin' has not arrived nor will it. I will always have time to sass you and everytime you leave me alone for five minutes I will work on my sultry southern looks if that's what makes your blood boil." She squeezed his fingers. He stopped in front of the elderly gentleman wearing overalls. He wasn't so very different than Jim Bob. Tall, lanky, and sparkling brown eyes. His hair was receding but there was an ancient youthfulness about his face. Square and few wrinkles, except around his eyes, and those were laugh lines.

"Now, Denison, you introduce me to this handsome gentleman," Retta teased. "And where is you wife?" she asked.

"Ada? Why she's the one with the pretty grey hair right over there." The man pointed to a lady in a denim jumper who was uncovering pots of food on a long, long table. "She can cook like an angel and sing like a saint. And if Denison's got a brain in his head, he'll hog-tie you and keep you right here in Bugtussle to fill her shoes when we're dead and gone."

Denison shook his head. "Quit talkin' like that Herman. You know you and Ada will be here when eternity dawns. Bugtussle couldn't live without you two."

"Hummmp," he snorted. "Got to go see what Ada needs." He waved across the room and disappeared.

"Now that Frank has proposed for you and I'm supposed to fill Ada's shoes, what have you got to say for yourself?" Retta asked, teasing aside and as serious as flying in a rainstorm.

"I'd say you and I better . . ."

"Dinner is ready. Herman will offer up thanks." Ada clapped her hands and got everyone's attention. "Then we can eat."

"Dinner won't always save you." Retta laughed, not quite sure if she was ready for some kind of serious commitment after all. Maybe this was just one of those survivor things which happened after a near-death experience. They'd survived it together and now they were clinging together out of fear of it happening again. When she was back in Nashville and he was safe on Gem's Acres, he might call her every night for a week, then slowly their relationship would die-in-its-sleep, and it would go to rest easier if they didn't make bold statements about love and plans for the future. Next year he might be married to Terri and she might be still fighting with the insurance company about the King's Star. She shivered just thinking about that red-haired witch touching Denison's ear again.

Chapter Twelve

Retta pretended to read a magazine in the commercial airliner on the way home to Nashville. The giddiness of survival had passed last night when Denison kissed her goodnight at the top of the stairs. The embrace didn't hold the passion or the excitement it had in the past. For the first time since she'd been at the ranch she pulled the wispy curtains shut and refused to look at the stars because they reminded her of her precious plane. The resolute way she'd come through the whole mess crumbled as she curled up in a ball on the bed.

Denison had dark circles under his eyes this morning at the breakfast table and even though Gem chattered on and on about Retta coming back to the ranch in a few weeks for another visit, Retta knew she felt the tension between them. When she hugged Retta goodbye she told her that everyone argued occasionally and to talk to Denison about the problem. Whatever he did to upset her could be fixed if they would just talk about it, she'd said.

But a problem had to be recognized before it could be fixed as Gem said. And there was no problem. They'd ridden the roller coaster called giddy survival for almost a week now. Like all rides, it had come to an end and there didn't seem to be anything past that. The kiss was flat as a pancake. Neither of them said five words on the way to the airport and now he sat with his magazine open in his lap as he stared out the window.

She wanted the flight to finish and get back into her routine. Routine. Tears welled up in her eyes at that word. She'd never known a time without the King's Star. Her father bought it the year before she was born in 1973 and she'd always known it would be hers. Now it was gone. Routine? How crazy! Routine would never, ever be the same again. She couldn't crop dust or help the fire department. Not unless she used her insurance money to purchase another plane, and with the cost of a good Cessna these days, she didn't even know if there would be enough funds to buy one.

She looked back over the week she'd spent at the ranch and tried to analyze the silly numbness in her heart. It should have been there in the beginning. From the time Jim Bob picked them up, she should have been in acute mourning for what she lost. But instead she acted like a sixteen-year-old kid who'd just walked away from a devastating automobile wreck. Instead of fear, she and Denison both went through days of feeling like they were invincible. They'd faced death, looked it right in the eyeball and spit in its face, and walked away practically unscathed.

The hollow spot in the middle of her chest didn't feel quite so cocky right that minute as she stared at the picture in the magazine without seeing anything. Auntie always told her that confidence was that cocky feeling a person had just before they fell flat on their face. At that moment, high above the world, sitting beside the most handsome man she'd ever know, Patsy Loretta King didn't have an ounce of confidence left in her small frame, let alone any form of cockiness. She was stretched out emotionally as flat on her face as she'd ever been in all her life.

Denison watched the blue sky, almost the same shade of color as Retta's eyes. Where had the glitter and glow been last night when he kissed her? The day had been a wonderful success. They'd spent hours sitting on a blanket on the edge of the lake, watching the water lap in and out, talking about everything from the stars of the Opry to Lila's wedding. From the time they left the Italian restaurant where they had supper until they got home something died.

He wanted to talk about it, but he didn't know where to begin. They'd both flirted and held each other and acted like two people desperately in love all week. Gem was floating around on clouds after the pot-luck dinner at the church when Retta had put Terri in her place. People died, he reminded himself. Sometimes they lingered on in sickness for years then finally breathed their last. Sometimes they went suddenly. One minute they were breathing, laughing, talking, planting crops and eating supper. The next day they were laying in a casket and friends and neighbors were weeping over their remains.

Relationships die the same way. At times they linger on trying to restore what had once been and others are over as quickly as a massive heart attack. But he didn't want the relationship to die. He wanted it to last through this life and into eternity.

"Want to talk about it?" he finally asked but he didn't reach across the armrest and take her hand in his. He didn't want to feel the coldness if there really was no life left in the whirlwind they'd been tied up in all week.

"There's nothing to say," she said emotionless without looking at his green eyes. She wanted to remember the twinkle when she teased him at the church social or the soft look when he laid her on the sofa in that travel-trailer. Someday when she was old and had her grey hair done at the beauty shop every week like Auntie did, she wanted to remember a week of wild abandonment. When her hair was purple one week she wanted to remember the violet in the Oklahoma sunset over the lake at Juniper Point when she caught a striper bass. When it was blue the next week she would think of the blue dress she wore to the church social, and when it was it's right color, the week when everything in the world was true and right would come to her mind.

Auntie met them at the gate, hugging Retta so tightly she could scarcely breath. "That may be your last trip up in the air," she declared. "I told your father when he was so took with flying that it would be the ruination of him. And it nearly took you away from me," she rambled. "I'm glad you're driving back to Bugtussle, Denison. Now let's pick up your bags and get you home. Denison has a gig tonight according to Lila and you've got a lot of paper work to get done. I've been in touch with the insurance people and that nice man, Red Hooligan or something like that, sent us some Polaroid picture shots of the plane. Mercy, girl, it's a wonder you two survived."

Retta crawled into the front seat with Anna, and Denison got into the back before Anna could say anything about him driving. An empty sadness filled his heart, but just as surely as he could not walk on water or resurrect a dead person, he could not breath life into the unity they seemed to have until last night. It was better to let it go and remember it with a smile than hang on just to be hanging on as one country artist wrote.

"Thanks for the ride, Miss Anna," he said when she drove him to the hangar where he'd left his truck. "I'll be going on to the apartment and getting my things packed. I think I'll go ahead and drive back today. If I get started soon, I can make it by midnight or a little after," he said as he got out of the backseat. "I'll see you in a little bit, Retta." He waved.

"Okay, what's going on?" Anna turned and demanded, her blue eyes flashing anger as she drove back toward the place where Retta lived. "Gem said something happened last night and you two both looked like warmed over sin before daylight this morning at breakfast. It's more than just not wanting to say goodbye to each other, so tell me what?"

"I don't know." Retta's eyes swimmed in pools of tears which spilled over her cheeks. "We were almost flighty all week. Then the bottom fell out. I should have come home right after it happened. That very next day."

"I see," Anna nodded. "Well, we'll see what happens this next week. I put the paperwork on your kitchen table," she pulled into the apartment complex parking lot right beside Denison's white truck. "Want me to come help you since it's pretty final when you get that done."

"No, I think I'd rather be alone." Retta leaned across the seat and kissed her aunt's cheek, leaving a smudge of tears on her make-up when she pressed her cheek to hers in a hug. "I love you, Auntie. I'll be at work on Monday morning. Sorry I didn't come on back and help you . . ."

"Oh, hush. You'll have me crying," Anna said. "I just knew you were going to get married and I'd get to see a baby before I died."

"Maybe you will," Retta said. "Just not one with black hair and dark green eyes."

She dropped her brand new suitcase on the floor and avoided the kitchen table. She didn't want to see the King's Star in the pictures. Not yet. Not until after Denison came to say goodbye. She'd gone into the funeral parlor when her parents were laid out in their caskets all alone the first time. She'd never told Auntie that she'd spent an hour sitting on the front seat of the chapel while her heart lay in shambles inside those two caskets. She went to the house and picked her up that morning and the two of them wept together, leaning on each other for support.

The pictures were going to be like that. Telling Denison goodbye wasn't going to be easy, either. But both were necessary. One was the final link with her father, the other was the final link with what she'd thought might be a match made far above the clouds and skies.

The doorbell rang sooner than she thought it might and she opened the door to find Denison. He hadn't changed clothes but he had put on a pair of sunglasses for which she was glad. She didn't want to look at his eyes. She didn't want him to look at the blank blue in hers but her sunglasses were laying on the sofa and it would be strange to pick them up at this point.

"Thank you again for saving my life," she broke the

silence. He was standing propped up against her door jamb, staring at her.

"Thank you for a lovely week. I'm sorry it couldn't last forever," he said.

"Some thing's burn a long time. Others burn out quickly," she said philosophically.

"Then this is goodbye?" He raised an eyebrow above the glasses.

She wanted to throw herself into his arms, however that would only prolong the inevitable. "I guess it is." She held out her hand to shake.

He shook his head. "Goodbye Retta," he whispered and turned away from her proffered hand.

She shut the door, stiffened her back, and went to the table. There it was in living color. Pictures of the burned out remains—no longer white with an electric blue stripe. No longer anything but the hull of metal with a tree imbedded in her tail end. Retta waited for the tears to come, but they didn't. Instead she saw her father trying to make her take the star from his hands and disappearing in a cloud of rain and smoke. Then she heard the soft thumping of Denison's heart as she laid her cheek against his chest when he carried her out of the storm.

She toyed with the star around her neck and the tears spilled out over her eyelashes, rolling down her face in rivers, and dripping off her jaw bone onto the collar of her shirt. She wasn't weeping for the plane. It was lifeless metal and the memories which were made in it, around it, and because of it could never be taken from her. Suddenly Retta remembered her mother talking about the first time her father took her up to the heavens before she could walk or utter a word. The last time she flew with her father before the accident—they flew to Little Rock to visit with Bud for the afternoon and then flew home in the evening. It was just for fun. There were all the trips in between. King's Star was gone, but no one could ever erase all the good times. No, she wasn't weeping for the airplane or even the loss of it that afternoon.

She wept for Denison.

She wept for the promise that hadn't been fulfilled, for the hope which didn't materialize, and for the love she wanted and couldn't have. She curled up in a ball on the couch, wiped away the tears with the back of her hand, and resolutely determined she wouldn't cry anymore. But it was futile. A fresh flow of tears streamed down her cheeks and she sobbed into the afghan on the back of the sofa.

In the middle of her tirade the phone rang and she reached for it, hoping that Denison was calling from the first pay phone he found to say he'd been wrong and that he wanted to climb back aboard the space shuttle they'd ridden to the moon and back several times in the past week. She wanted him to grab her in a bear hug and hold her close so she could hear the soft beating of his heart again.

"Hello," she said.

"Retta, darlin'," Brett said. "I'm so glad you are home and that you survived that horrible crash. I told you that you didn't have any business in that little mosquito. If a person has to fly they should at least go in jets. Those things aren't safe. I'm taking you to dinner tonight and I won't take no for an answer. Put on your best dancing shoes and we'll do the Southfork."

"No thank you," she said flatly.

"I said I won't take no," Brett demanded.

"And I said no," she told him. "I'm not going out with you Brett. I'm staying in all weekend and . . ."

"You're going to be sorry," Brett said. "This is your last chance."

"Probably," she said. "But the answer is still no."

"Are you ever going to change your mind about singers?"

"Yep, I already did. But I don't like you Brett, not because you're a singer, but because I don't like you . . . period," she said.

"You're a cold-hearted witch," he snorted before he hung up.

"Some say so," she muttered and grabbed her afghan to catch the next bunch of tears.

Chapter Thirteen

On Saturday morning she put on a pair of worn, faded jeans, and an old, grey sweatshirt and went to the cemetery. She sat down on the cold ground and tried to make sense of the past two months, from the time Denison walked into the flower shop until the time he left her apartment without even touching her hand.

"Momma," she said scarcely above a whisper, "I need some advice. What do I do now?"

"You've got to listen to your heart Retta. We want you to sing, but you don't want any part of it. We can't force it on you," memories of her mother's soft voice popped into her head.

"This has nothing to do with singing, Momma," Retta said aloud, not even caring that there were other people visiting gravesites only a few feet away. "It's got to do with whether or not we were just swept up in the moment. Glad to be alive."

"Listen to your heart, Retta . . ." was the message again.

"Daddy," she ran her finger over his name engraved into the grey marble. "What did you mean with that star in your hand? Take this, study the moment, and don't lose the best star you'll ever have," she repeated the words.

But nothing, not even a memory of him sitting in the cockpit of the plane, or telling her stories of Vietnam came to her mind. All she could see was him holding the star out to her and saying those words.

"Study what?" she rose from the ground, brushed the grass from the seat of her jeans and drove to Lila's house.

"Oh, Retta, I'm so glad you're here. Thank goodness you're alive. Now come in here and help me decide which shade to do the bouquets in. Should I use more electric blue or ecru? Remember now I've got eight bridemaids as well as a maid of honor, which of course is you, so think of eight bouquets lined up at the front of the church. Should we make big, droopy ones or little nosegays? I picked out a cake this week and can't wait for you to see the picture. Drop your coat on the chair and come in the living room. I've got things strewn from here to you, but it'll probably be that way until the wedding is over," Lila prattled.

"I can't stay," Retta didn't remove her jacket. "We'll have to look at the flowers another day. I just wanted to run by." She took off her sunglasses to wipe a stain from the lens.

"Good grief, Retta, what in the world have you been doing? Did you hurt your eyes in the crash? You've got to get some eye make-up on before you go out in public. You look like you've been on a three-day crying bender. Surely you didn't cry for that silly airplane. It's just a piece of machinery. You can always buy another one with the money you get from insurance," Lila told her.

"Yes, I can," Retta nodded. "Got to run for now though. Call me next week and we'll work on colors. I've got a thousand things to do right now. I just wanted to run by and touch base before I go back to work on Monday."

"Denison called me and said he was going home for good. There's a young kid filling in for him at the Opry for the next few nights and then Norman will be back. I bet you about died of boredom having to spend a whole week at that remote ranch—and with Denison, who you hate. You poor, poor baby," Lila crooned. "Well, call me when you've got a free minute. We'll do lunch and talk about roses or daisies or orchids."

"Sure thing," Retta waved.

* * *

On Saturday morning, Denison arose early. He'd gotten home after everyone was already sleeping and let himself into the house quietly. He'd made the trip in record time, stopping only for gas and a bag of chips to eat as he drove. He plugged a Vince Gill tape into the cassette player in his truck, and kept time to the music by tapping his fingers on the steering wheel. When the tape ended, he didn't know a single thing he'd heard. All he could think about was the vacant look in Retta's eyes when he looked at her. It was as if she couldn't wait for him to turn his back and walk away. It was as if she was on her own territory now and she didn't need him or his back-country ways any more.

He slept poorly in spite of being bone tired from such a long drive, and awoke before anyone was up and about. He dressed in faded jeans and a worn sweatshirt and made himself a cup of instant coffee. He grabbed his fishing poles and went to the lake where he and Retta fished a few days before. He threw his line out into the water, watched the red-and-white bobble bounce in the waves and tried to make his mind go completely blank and not think of Retta or the accident. He tried to think of nothing. But it didn't work.

On Monday morning she was at the flower shop at the same time Anna opened the doors. She'd taken Lila's advice and applied a little make-up to her swollen eyes, but Anna wasn't fooled one bit. "Are you finished mourning or do we need to make a funeral wreath this morning?"

"For the plane?"

"What else would we make a wreath for?" Anna snipped, fully aware of what she meant. "For the love of the lifetime which you tossed in the trash?"

"Oh, Auntie," Retta laid her head on her forearms on the work table in the back room. "What am I going to do? I went to the cemetery thinking maybe Momma or Daddy could help me. I thought maybe a bit of something they said in the past would trigger a response and I would know what to do. All I got from Momma was something about listening to my heart, and I had this strange dream about Daddy trying to hand me a star and telling me to study it or I might be throwing away the best star I ever had. How could I throw away a star? I went to Lila's and she's so involved with her wedding she doesn't have time to listen to me, and I don't know what to do."

"Hummmph," Anna snorted loudly. "Tell me who you're not going to date, marry, have a relationship with or anything else."

"I'm over that now, Auntie. I promise I'll look at the person and not judge them by other folk's mistakes." She looked up at her short great aunt, standing with both hands on her hips and a gleam in her eye.

"Just tell me . . . okay?"

"I didn't want anything to do with anyone who was

trying to be a star," Retta said, understanding even in a small measure finally dawning.

"Study the situation and don't throw it away," Anna repeated the jest of the words her father had said. "Now what on earth caused you two to fall off the clouds anyway?"

"I don't know. We just did." Retta fingered the star around her neck. The star fell . . . the King's Star fell . . . and Denison was going to be a star, but he went home to Oklahoma . . . so he fell. Catch me a real falling star, she used to say when her father asked what she wanted.

"Explain it to me," Anna said.

"We were coming home from dinner and suddenly everything got quiet and a pall fell over the truck and—I don't know how to explain it. He kissed me goodnight and the magic was gone, Auntie. There was no pizazz, just a flat kiss."

"Do all kisses have to have pizazz?" Anna asked.

"I can't make sense out of it," Retta admitted, trying to fit the pieces of the puzzle together in her heart. An airplane fell . . . Denison went home. She was miserable. She'd cried until her eyes were swollen and her heart was still in pieces.

"Then study it while I go to get us some doughnuts. I'll be back in an hour or so. I've got a couple of stops to make along the way. Think about what you just told me and I bet you find the answer in your heart, my child." She kissed Retta on the cheek and disappeared out the front door.

Retta picked up a pot of tulips, bright red, the harbinger of spring. Someone at the greenhouse had planted them in a plastic pot and kept them warm enough to bloom. When she got them wrapped in colorful paper with a big red bow, someone else would come in with a touch of early spring fever and take them home. She cut a piece of paper and set the pot in the middle of it and flipped wide red ribbon around her fingers until she had a ten loop bow made.

Work was what she needed. Lots of good hard work to make her forget all about that wonderful week when she threw caution to the wind and let her heart have full reign. "Well, well," Brett startled her so badly she jumped. "What have we here?"

"The coldest witch in the state," she snapped.

"Oh, let's kiss and make up," he drew her close and planted a kiss on her lips before she could protest. It wasn't bad but it wasn't even as good as the one Denison gave her that last night. She pushed him away and wiped her mouth with the back of her hand.

"You *are* cold." Brett laughed. "I thought you'd want to be the first one to kiss the groom. Celeste and I are engaged as of last night. We are planning a July wedding. Right after Lila's. Of course, nothing quite that elaborate, but still a show for the media."

"And you're in here kissing me?" she asked incredulously.

"Just giving you one last chance to change my mind." He shook a finger under her nose. "We would have been the duet of the year. Awards, tuxedoes, fancy dresses, the whole works."

Retta just shook her head and frowned. "I hope you are both very happy," she said.

"Oh, we will be," Brett nodded. "We're going to knock them all dead. We're already working on a duet that is destined to be the next number-one best-seller. See you around, Retta." He didn't give her time to answer as he fanned past the counter and out the door.

She picked up a pot of pink tulips and cocked her head to one side. The pretty pink paper was right there and the hot pink ribbon from the Christmas poinsettia which caused all the stir amongst the make-up convention women. She ripped off a piece of paper and set the pot in the middle of it. Her hands were tied up in ribbon when she felt rather than heard a presence behind her. If that rotten Brett had come back to try one more last time to seduce her, she intended to slap him silly with a roll of ribbon. She turned quickly— a sharp lecture on the end of her tongue—to find Denison standing so close she gasped.

"That's really pretty, its like the one you made at Christmas when I first met you, isn't it?" he said, his green eyes boring into hers.

"Yes, it is," she said, amazed that she could utter a sound. "What can I do for you today? A dozen roses for your Darlin' Emma?"

"You need to get that doorbell fixed," he said just above a whisper as he reached out and touched her shoulder and sparks danced all over the flower shop. He ran a fore finger down her face, stopping to outline her lips and chill bumps the size of the mountain where the King's Star was buried, raised up on her arms and neck.

"Yes, we do." She was mesmerized by the look on his handsome face and the touch of his hand on her skin.

He took a step forward and folded her up in his arms in a hug that shook her heart like an earthquake. Then he tilted back her chin and kissed her—long, deep and passionately.

And the pizazz was there.

"Oh, my," she mumbled and pulled his mouth down for another searing kiss.

"What can you do for me today?" he said when she leaned back and looked at him again.

"Yes, sir," she nodded. "A basket of tulips. A rose in a vase?"

"You can marry me," he said.

A thousand bells went off at the same time, alarm clocks, school bells, train–whistles, Christmas bells. She shut her eyes and a star fell from the sky and her father caught it in the palm of his hand and held it out to her. She knew beyond any shadow of doubt that the star was just a symbol of Denison Adams.

"Yes," she said. "I will marry you. I don't care if

you write songs and imitate Bill Anderson for the rest of your life. I don't care if you manage the ranch and we live in Bugtussle until we die and they bury us in the cemetery right there. I don't ever want to be away from you again. I'm miserable without you."

"Me, too," he said simply as he looked deeply into her eyes and there was only stars of love dancing in the depths of all that blue.

Chapter Fourteen

Retta looked at her reflection in the floor-length mirror in her bedroom at the ranch. The long, sheath dress fit her to perfection and the circlet of white roses twisted around the curls on top of her head was just what she wanted. She didn't want a veil to interfere with the kiss at the end of the ceremony or to get tangled up in the cake icing. She stopped to smell the dozen roses on the dresser. Red ones delivered this morning with a card which read, *I'd give you the moon and stars if it were in my power. I love you, Denison.*

Anna poked her head in the door, "Oh my aren't you beautiful. And the roses," she sighed. "I couldn't have made them better myself. Turn around now and let me fasten the necklace for you. You'll get it all wrapped up in your hair. You should see the wedding ring. Did Denison tell you about it yet?"

"No, I told him to surprise me. I just didn't want

two rings. I don't want to be engaged. I want to be married," Retta told her. "Is it pretty?"

"If you want to be surprised then I'm not telling secrets," Anna laughed. "You met that good-looking doctor yet?"

"Yep," Retta nodded. "And as far as I know he doesn't have a bunch of kids you'd have to raise."

"Oh, hush, your mouth," Anna actually blushed as she kissed her one last time on the cheek. "The preacher is down there and they'll be starting the music in ten minutes." Anna checked her watch.

Was she doing the right thing? After all it had only been three months since she first laid eyes on Denison Adams. And the first two of those she'd worked hard to convince herself she didn't even like him. She'd been at the ranch for almost a month now, flying back with Jim Bob and Denison on the very day he proposed. She loved him with her whole heart or at least she thought she did. But right that minute she wished she was one of those magnificent eagles and could sweep out the window to a high perch to think just a few more minutes about what she was doing.

"Jitters?" Gem slipped through the door. "Thought I'd run in for a minute. Got something blue and borrowed and all that stuff. I remember when I married Denison's grandfather. Mercy me, all I wanted to do was bolt and tear off down the pasture like a jack rabbit. I couldn't breath. I could barely say my vows and . . ."

"What did you do?" Retta's eyes were wide with wonder.

"I married him. I looked up in those big old green eyes and saw just as much fear in them as I had in mine, and all I could think about was that we had enough love to smother the fear." Gem laughed. "And we did. Fifty years of marriage. Denison's dad and mom just got here. As usual, almost late. But they brought her mother along. Darling Emma. Wait 'til you meet her. She's the strangest bird you'll ever meet and with a good old solid name like Emma. I should have got her name and she should have gotten mine. Gem!" Granny rolled her eyes. "Momma said Daddy wanted a boy and Jim was the only name he liked. So she just adjusted the spelling and he had a Gem. Emma is the one in the gypsy-looking outfit and lots of silver jewelry. She dotes on Denison and I saw her give him a folded check for a wedding gift. Probably enough to buy the whole state of Texas," she whispered.

"I'm glad they're here," Retta said. "But I've got to admit, Granny, I'm about half afraid to meet them."

"Don't be. Amelia is odd like Emma and has the money to support it. She couldn't spend in two life times what her father left her, and my son is almost as much in love with her after thirty years of marriage as he was the day he met her, almost as much as Denison is with you. Thank goodness you've got a good head on your shoulders and your feet rooted in common sense. If you tried to cart off Denison I'd probably lay down and die," Gem said. "I hear the music starting up. When this song is finished then the preacher's wife will start the old here comes the bride stuff. Ready?"

"I think so, thanks to you," Retta leaned over and lightly kissed Gem on the forehead then wiped away the light pink lipstick stain.

She waited inside the bedroom until she heard the first strains of the traditional song and then stepped out onto the landing, walking slowly down each step. She carried a bouquet of white roses laying in a bed of fern and tied with a long, white satin ribbon. The train attached to the back of her gown weighed a ton, or so she thought as she pulled it down the stairs behind her. Auntie and Gem could unhook it after the wedding ceremony and before they went to the church for the reception. Then she'd just be wearing the simple brocade dress with a scoop neckline and long, fitted sleeves ending at a point on the top of her hands.

When she reached the bottom of the steps, Denison reached out his hand and led her to the archway in front of the preacher. Without letting go of her hand he began the ceremony. "We are glad everyone could join us this day for our wedding vows," he said to the few family members behind them and then looked into her eyes. "Patsy Loretta King, I want to be your husband from this day forth. I want to celebrate life with you everyday. I vow to do all that is in my power, both financially, emotionally, and physically to make you happy all the days of your life."

"Denison Edward Adams, I want to be your wife from this day forward. I will celebrate life with you everyday, whether in joy or sorrow. I give you my vow to do all that is in my power to make you happy forever," Retta said in a loud clear voice.

She heard Auntie sniffle and the preacher clear his throat, "Dearly beloved, we are gathered here today in the sight of our Heavenly Father and these family members. He looked up at Thomas and Matthew sitting with their wives and daughters, at Gem who was beaming, Anna King, who wiped a tear from her eye, and at Frank, who looked so much like an older Denison, and Amelia, the exotic-looking woman with the blackest hair he'd ever seen and the greenest eyes, who had to be Denison's mother. He looked at the tall lady in the gypsy outfit sitting beside Denison's mother. Gem told him it was Emma, the other grandmother from Tulsa. He could certainly tell where the daughter got her peculiarity.

There was not a lot of family but they were a joyous, accepting lot. He cleared his throat one more time and began the traditional wedding up to and including a very sweet kiss at the end. Gem and Anna both wondered, since it was so short, if it had pizazz.

The reception was held both inside the fellowship hall of the Bugtussle Baptist Church and out on the lawn. Lace tableclothes covered the tables with centerpieces of roses and trailing ivy. Children in their Sunday best played hide-and-go-seek and tag in wild abandonment around the church. Inside the fellowship hall, Denison and Retta cut the cake and fed each other while the photographer's flash lit up the room, recording the ceremony for all future generations to see in years to come.

Gem Adams clinked a spoon on a crystal glass to get everyone's attention. "We are glad each and every one of you are here today to join us in this joyous celebration. The cake is ready to be cut but before you partake, you might want to enjoy the food outside. Jim Bob has barbecued a steer and Martha's been cooking for a week. There's food enough to feed all of Bugtussle. So grab a plate and enjoy right after Dr. Linsell says grace for us."

"Ahem," the doctor cleared his throat and delivered thanksgiving for the beautiful spring day, the food, and the married couple.

"Can you believe she'd actually barbecued beef and there are tables full of food. This looks like a backcountry pot-luck supper, not a formal wedding," Lila sniffed to Samuel, who just patted her arm and laughed.

"Now, Lila. Not everyone has your flair for a party or a reception. If this is what Denison and Retta want, then be happy for them. She'll be happy at your wedding this summer even though it'll be different from this," he chided gently.

"Okay," she sighed, "and you can bet your boots and half next year's salary, it'll be different. Barbecue! And kids running around like hoodlums," she snorted but she put on a big smile and went outside to find Retta who was first in the food line.

"Oh, honey, your dress is just exquisite. And I love the simplicity of the bouquet. But who was your maid of honor? Oh, do be careful and don't get that horrid red sauce on your dress," Lila shivered at the thought.

"Okay." She giggled. Lila was just Lila. One did not change a leopard's spots, but that didn't mean you couldn't love the leopard just the way it was. "We didn't have one or a best man either," Retta told her. "It was just a simple ceremony with only family and then this reception. We had Auntie and Gem sign as witnesses. I guess that makes Auntie a maid of honor and Gem the best man, doesn't it? Isn't it wonderful, Lila? I love it. I love this little church. It's so warm and friendly. Did you see the cows in the pasture over there and just look at those beautiful mountains?"

"Yes, I did, but I'd rather stay inside. I can't see you living here forever," Lila exclaimed. "I can't believe you're leaving the city and a career in singing."

"I never had a career in singing," Retta laughed.

"But you could have. You've given it all up for this backwater existence," Lila whined.

"I gave it all up for the love of my life," Retta said.

"Well, he might have a very rewarding career in song writing and you could still live in Nashville. Besides," she leaned forward and whispered in Retta's ear. "I know there's enough money in the mother's side, that all he'd have to do is say the word and she'd buy him a recording studio of his own."

"But that's not what we want," Denison overheard just enough to know what she'd said. "We love Bugtussle. We love the ranch and we're staying right here. When the fast pace of the city gets too much for you, come on down and visit us," he said. "Go get Thomas and sit beside us while we devour this food. I bet Retta is hungry enough to eat a bear right now," he said teasing her.

"You got that right." Retta nodded. "Claws, growl and even hide, and I wouldn't even snarl my nose at the smell."

Later that evening, Anna and the doctor were admiring her wedding ring and she realized Denison wasn't beside her. She scanned the room and Denison raised a hand and winked at her from the doorway. That was her cue. The absolute perfect moment had arrived. When he winked she was to make her way to the door, toss her bouquet, and they would ride off into the beautiful sunset together. "I'm fixing to throw the flowers," she whispered conspiratorially to Lila as she passed her on the way to the door to leave with her brand-new husband.

"I don't need them. I'm already engaged and getting

married soon," Lila smiled. "Let one of these plain country women have them. They'll need all the help they can get."

Retta just smiled.

Denison draped his arm around her shoulder when she reached him. "Thank you all for coming to the reception," he announced in a big, booming voice which brought instant silence. "We're leaving now. I promised my bride that when the sun was just an orange ball on the horizon we would ride off into the sunset together. Just like in all the love stories. Stay around and enjoy the food and fellowship. Jim Bob says there's still half a steer outside, so if you don't want to eat any more then get a plate and take some home for dinner tomorrow. We'll see you Sunday morning in church."

Retta tossed the bouquet over her shoulder and it floated above Lila's head and right into Anna's arms. She held it up like a trophy. "I'm next," she announced. "There isn't any small print about age, is there?"

"No, ma'am," the doctor declared at her elbow.

Denison opened the door of the cabin on the shore of the lake and carried his new bride over the threshold, kissing her the whole time, not even breaking it off when he set her down. He reached around behind her and shut the door, then leaned back to look at her beaming expression. It was so very different from that day he carried her from the burning plane to the travel-trailer.

She looked past his face and at her hand which she'd slung around his neck. There on her ring finger was a solitaire diamond set on a wide gold band, sparkling in the light of a dozen candles he'd ordered lit at a certain time so they'd be glowing when they arrived. If she dropped her hand just slightly the gleam looked like a falling star.

"Like it?" he asked.

"Love it," she said. "I'm glad I let you pick it out and surprise me with it."

"I tried to get one cut in the shape of a star." He drew her close to him and she laid her head on his chest, listening to the steady rhythm. "But . . ."

"This is perfect. It glitters like a falling star," she said. "You're my real star, Denison. You're the one I've waited for all my life and nearly let fall all the way to earth before I woke up and realized what I was about to miss. I love you with my whole heart."

"I love you, too, my darling. Now I know what real magic is and it has nothing to do with neon rainbows and glass awards. It's what we've got together. And what we've got isn't ever going to burn out, Retta Adams. It's going to burn forever just like a bright star," he said simply and kissed her again just as a star shot across the sky right outside the cabin's window. Neither of them saw it.